THE RANCHER'S FIERY BRIDE

MONTANA WESTWARD BRIDES BOOK 0

AMELIA ROSE

CONTENTS

This book is dedicated to all of my faithful readers, without whom I would be nothing. I thank you for the support, reviews, love, and friendship you have shown me as we have gone through this journey together. I am truly blessed to have such a wonderful readership.

CHAPTER 1

*B*irdsong filled the early late August air as Mason Crawford drove his buggy into town. Pretty, wispy clouds drifted across a crystalline blue sky and a cool, gentle breeze played through the trees and bushes that lined the road. However, all this natural beauty was lost on Mason because his mind was focused on what was about to happen.

In perhaps three-quarters of an hour, he would meet the future Mrs. Crawford. Miss Jenny Carson would be arriving in Spruce Valley, Montana Territory, on the three o'clock stagecoach, and Mason's life would change forever. The question was whether it would change for the better or the worse.

Marrying a mail-order bride hadn't been Mason's idea. Heck, marrying at all hadn't been his idea. No, his Aunt Cecilia and Uncle Herb had been the orchestrators of the whole affair. Frowning, Mason wondered yet again how he'd let the old couple talk him into getting hitched to a stranger. He'd tried to explain to them that he was happy just as he was, but they'd refused to listen to him.

They'd argued with him about it until finally telling him that they wouldn't leave the Circle C Ranch to him when they passed on unless he got married. The ranch was Mason's life, the place he imagined spending the rest of his life. He'd planned on getting married sooner or later, but he hadn't been in a rush. He had plenty of time, didn't he?

His aunt and uncle obviously didn't think so. Aunt Cecilia had urged him to have children while he was young enough to enjoy them, as though twenty-nine was old. As he remembered the conversation, Mason let out a snort without being aware of it, and his horse's ears flicked back at the sound.

Trepidation and dismay made his chest feel a little tight when Frost's Station & Eatery came into view as he rounded a turn.

People shopped at the mercantile and ate in the little restaurant that took up the back third of the building. Both the stagecoach and the mail coach stopped there, and it was where many informal town meetings occurred. In fact, it was the busiest place in the small town. There were even a few rooms over the store that people could rent. Outside of Mrs. Snyder's, it was the only place where visitors who didn't have family in the area could stay.

Pulling up in front of the Station, as the townsfolk called it, Mason felt a little relieved to see that the stagecoach hadn't arrived quite yet. It gave him a few minutes to become more resigned to the fact that he'd be a married man within a week. Looking across the street at the small, white clapboard building that stood empty, he admitted that Miss Carson coming to Spruce Valley would solve another problem besides providing him with a spouse.

Shortly before the end of the school year that spring, Mr. Bixby, the schoolteacher, had passed away from a heart attack, leaving the area youngsters without a teacher. As in many other communities in the territory, the ranchers and farmers of Spruce Valley often relied on their older children to help with the workload, but most of the citizens agreed that their kids should also receive an education.

So, when Mason had told his aunt that one of the women who'd answered his advertisement was a former governess, she'd insisted that he set his sights on her. Mason wasn't a vain or superficial man, but he figured that a woman's looks were something that should be considered when getting married. Committing to a woman he hadn't seen didn't appeal at all to him.

Therefore, he'd sent Miss Carson a picture and had received one in return. The sepia picture had made it difficult to tell Jenny's hair color, but she'd informed him that she had red hair and blue eyes. She had a pretty smile, and her letters reflected a pleasant-tempered, intelligent woman.

After a couple more letters, Mason had asked her to come to Spruce Valley to marry him. He'd half-hoped she'd refuse but, alas, she'd accepted. And she'd be there in a matter of minutes.

Mason sighed as he wrapped the lines around the brake handle and jumped out of the buggy. He nodded to a few people he knew as he stepped onto the wide porch that ran the length of the storefront and doubled as the stagecoach depot. As he entered the establishment, the scents of fresh-baked bread and savory meat made his stomach growl.

Conversation flowed through the store, and carried over from the restaurant, too. Smiling when he heard a couple of kids laugh somewhere in the store as he approached the counter, Mason greeted Damon Frost, the owner of the Station.

"So, today's the day," Damon greeted him, his large, graying walrus mustache twitching as he smiled.

Mason nodded. "Yep. Sure is."

Damon's dark eyes twinkled. "Nervous, son?"

Mason met the portly, elderly man's gaze. "Not nervous, more like I've accepted it."

Damon guffawed and reached across the counter to thump Mason's shoulder. "Now, now. This is a good thing. You'll see. Don't know what I'd have done all these years without my Maggie."

Mason felt a rush of affection for one of his favorite people. Maggie Frost was, indeed, a special woman, and she and Damon were always amusing when they were together. "Well, she's one of a kind," he remarked. "I have no idea what Miss Carson is really like."

"Give her a chance, Mason. I'm sure she's just as nervous as you are, coming to a strange place like this," Damon said. "Be the gentleman that Cecilia and Herb raised you to be."

"Yes, sir," Mason agreed. "I reckon you're right." He motioned at several wildflower arrangements in a large basket that sat on a stand close to the counter. "In fact, I'd like to get her one of those. And are there any tables free in the back? I figure that she's gonna be plum starving when she gets here."

"Good thinking," Damon said. "Elmarie just brought those flowers in, so they're nice and fresh. I'll make sure that a table is clear for you."

"Much obliged," Mason said as he counted out some coins and handed them to Damon.

The bunch of flowers was priced less than he'd given, but fourteen-year-old Elmarie Harmon, who picked and sold the flowers, was trying to help support a sick mother and two younger brothers. Mason could afford a little extra to make things a little easier for the Harmons.

The sound of wheels, rapid hoofbeats, and squeaking springs announced the arrival of the stagecoach. Mason's stomach dropped. Despite his statement to Damon, he did feel apprehensive. He was also surprised to find himself hoping that Miss Carson would like him, almost as much as he hoped he would like her.

With a tight smile to Damon, he took up the bouquet, carrying it almost as if it was a shield, and headed out the door to meet his intended.

CHAPTER 2

*A*s the conveyance slowed to a halt, Jenny Carson did her best to freshen her appearance. It was no simple task after the hot, dusty ride that had seemed endless. Not only had the stagecoach been uncomfortable, but her traveling companions were unbelievably tedious. Mrs. Timmons, a shrewish, elderly woman, and her equally unpleasant son, Gary, had argued almost the entire way from the last stop just before they'd crossed into the Montana Territory.

Finally, at around noon, Jenny hadn't been able to contain her frustration any longer and had shouted at them to cease their incessant bickering. Mother and son had traded shocked remarks about Jenny's behavior before going silent. Blessed peace had reigned in the coach for the rest of the trip until the stagecoach driver had shouted down to them that they'd reach Spruce Valley within fifteen minutes.

Jenny's head still hurt from their shrill voices and she thought she'd go insane from it. When the coach came to a final standstill, the Timmons pair wasted no time in disembarking. Jenny let her eyes drift shut for a few moments while she prepared to embark and meet her future husband.

The one blessing that had come from the churlish pair was that they'd largely distracted her from being nervous about coming to Spruce Valley. She rubbed her right temple as she took a deep breath and thought how wonderful some cool water would taste. Her eyes popped open when she remembered that she was about to meet her future husband. How could she have forgotten that?

Jenny smoothed the skirt of her powder blue muslin dress, collected her reticule and small embroidered carpetbag, and started for the stagecoach door. She gasped and took a hasty step backward when a man popped his head inside. Her legs bumped against the seat she'd just vacated, and she almost fell backward onto it.

At the last moment, she caught herself and glared at the man. "Do you always go around startling people like that?" she demanded.

Even though his cheeks turned a little pink, his mouth curved upwards in a smile. "Sorry about that, ma'am. I meant no harm."

Mollified by his apology, Jenny took a step toward the door. "Very well."

"Are you Miss Carson?"

"Why, yes, I am."

The man's smile broadened as he stepped back from the door. "In that case, allow me to introduce myself. I'm Mason Crawford, the man you came to marry."

Jenny's eyes widened, and her heartbeat leaped at his pronouncement. Her stomach knotted with sudden nerves. Her gaze roamed over his face, and she was surprised by what she saw. She should have been able to recognize Mason from his picture, but the image hadn't done the man justice.

While the photograph had shown a rather handsome man, it hadn't accurately depicted his chiseled cheekbones, fine straight nose, and strong jaw. His smile drew her attention to his sensual, masculine mouth that stirred thoughts of kissing him in her mind. His dove gray eyes gleamed with amusement.

He held out a hand. "Let me take your bag."

Jenny drew her thoughts together. "Oh, yes. Thank you."

Mason took her bag and then gave her his free hand. "What say we get you out of there and get some food into you? I'm sure you're ready for some vittles."

His rough palm against hers turned the knot in her stomach into a fluttering bird as he assisted her out of the coach.

"She's got two trunks here, Mason," Ted Drayton informed the rancher.

Mason frowned but said, "That's fine. They should fit in the back of the buggy." His gaze turned to Jenny. "Aunt Cecilia insisted that I bring it instead of the wagon, so the ride home was easier on your behind."

His teasing smile made it impossible for Jenny to take offense at his inappropriate remark. She'd heard far worse from her older brothers.

She arched an eyebrow and assumed a haughty air. "I'll thank you to not worry about my behind, Mr. Crawford."

Her tone made him chuckle. "Duly noted."

Ted handed Jenny's small trunks down to Mason and he loaded them in the buggy. He secured them with a leather strap to keep them from bouncing around. Jenny had brought a couple of things that were fragile and was glad that he was being careful with her belongings.

With a hand behind his back, Mason returned and held a bouquet of flowers out to her. "For you."

Touched by his thoughtful gesture, Jenny gave him a bright smile as she accepted the bouquet. Closing her eyes, she inhaled the fresh, calming scent of lavender and daisies. Her anxiety melted away, and she opened her eyes to find Mason studying her.

"Thank you very much. They're lovely," she said.

A relieved smile enhanced his handsomeness, and Jenny was hard-pressed not to stare.

"You're welcome. Well, how about those refreshments?"

Jenny chided herself over being so starry-eyed and regained her composure. "That sounds heavenly."

She took the arm that Mason offered her and let him lead her toward the mercantile. It was a cheerful, if slightly odd-looking, structure. The front half of the building resembled most other general stores, but the back half was a few feet shorter and narrower. She didn't have time to examine it in detail before they arrived at the front door. Mason opened it for her and motioned her inside.

Rows of straight wooden shelving stretched out before her. To the left stood the counter, upon which sat a thick ledger. A large, black pot-bellied stove was situated in the corner closest to the counter and several wooden chairs were arranged around it. It was evident that the store owner took pride in their establishment. Everything was clean and orderly.

While Jenny was busy looking around, Mason studied her. Her crimson hair was swept back in a high chignon that showed off her small, delicate ears and pretty neck. Although curly tendrils of hair had come loose, they didn't detract from her appearance. A few freckles dotted the bridge of her slightly pert nose, under which her pretty mouth was curved in a small smile. Mason was glad to see that Jenny wasn't petite or frail. Her dress hinted at lush curves that he could well-imagine would feel good in a man's arms.

"So, she's here!"

Mason jerked his eyes from Jenny at the sound of Damon's voice. The store owner strode up the center aisle, his face lit up in a big smile.

"Miss Carson, this is my good friend Damon Frost. He owns the Station," Mason said. "Damon, this is Miss Jenny Carson."

Damon held out a hand to her. "Nice to meet you, Miss Carson. Welcome to Spruce Valley. I hope you had a good trip."

Jenny gave him her hand and smiled. "How do you do, Mr. Frost? Thank you for asking. The trip was fine, if rather long." She didn't see the need to inform them about the unpleasant company of the Timmons.

"Is there a table ready in the back?" Mason asked. "I'm sure Miss Carson is thirsty and hungry."

"Of course." Damon motioned for them to follow him. "Right this way."

As they walked down the center aisle, Jenny noted the quality merchandise Damon sold. Various tools, household items, and even toys lined the shelves. As they emerged from the store portion of the building, mouth-watering scents reached Jenny and she began to feel a little faint with hunger.

The restaurant wasn't fancy, but it was clean with pretty curtains at the large windows and red checkered tablecloths covering the tables. The hardwood floors were scuffed, indicating that many feet had walked on them.

Damon led them to a table in a corner away from the windows, which Jenny appreciated. It would be cooler there, out of the sun. Mason pulled out a chair for her and she allowed him to seat her. She took the white napkin from in front of her and spread it across her lap as Mason took his seat across from her.

She watched him take off his tan hat, which he sat on the empty chair to his right. She noticed that his black hair was clean and looked like it had been recently trimmed, even though it still brushed his shoulders.

"Nell will be along in two shakes of a lamb's tail to get your order," Damon said. "She doesn't let any grass grow under her feet."

Jenny smiled at his proud tone as he left them.

"So, I saw the Timmons get off before you did. Your trip couldn't have been all that good if you had to ride with them for any length of time."

Jenny blinked a couple of times, surprised by his remark. "You know them?"

Mason nodded. "Yep. They come to stay with Mrs. Timmons' brother, Edgar James, about this time every year. They visit for a month and then head back East. I'm not sure why they come since they're always complaining about it here, but it's really none of my business."

Jenny noticed that several of the other diners kept

glancing at her and Mason. "It's not just this town they complain about," she said. "They complain about everything; the weather, the squeaky coach wheels, the sun is too hot, the wind is too cold…"

Mason's warm chuckle interrupted her, and Jenny couldn't resist a giggle at the twinkle in his eyes.

"You already know them well," he said.

The arrival of a woman Jenny assumed to be Nell prevented further conversation. Mason's next remark confirmed her supposition.

"Nell Danvers, this is Miss Jenny Carson."

Nell, a short woman who appeared to be in her late thirties, gave Jenny a tight smile. "Nice to meet you, ma'am. Mason, good to see you. What'll it be?"

Her rather brusque attitude didn't seem to bother Mason, so Jenny decided not to take offense. "How do you do, Nell? I'd love some lemonade and a cold lunch of some sort. What do you recommend?" she asked.

Nell drew herself up, seeming proud to have been asked. "Well, how about a nice big sandwich? We have some real good ham and some nice cheddar cheese from Liddy Bentley. She makes the best cheese in these parts. Anson's bread is especially tasty today, and we have pickled cabbage. How does that sound?"

Mason wondered if this was the same woman he'd known all his life. It was rare that Nell said more than ten words at a time.

Jenny hoped neither Nell nor Mason could hear her stomach growl. "It sounds wonderful. Thank you."

This time, Nell's smile was genuine. "You're welcome." Her expression cooled. "Your usual, Mason?"

Mason mumbled, "Uh, yeah. That's fine."

With a brief nod, Nell walked away. Mason made sure she was out of earshot before he asked, "How the heck did you do that?"

Jenny's eyebrows rose. "Do what?"

"Get her to talk so much and look so happy," Mason replied.

Perplexed, Jenny shook her head a little. "I don't know what you mean. I was just being friendly. And she asked what we wanted before I even knew what they serve here, so it was just easier to ask for her recommendation."

Mason rubbed his chin and pondered for a few moments. "Maybe it's because you're new. Most of us around here know what's on the menu, so we don't ask about it like you did."

Jenny smoothed her napkin over her lap. "Perhaps what you mistake for reticence on Nell's part is merely boredom. It must be very tedious for her if everyone orders the same thing day in and day out."

Looking at it from that perspective, Mason had to agree with her. It had never occurred to him that Nell might be bored. Of course, he didn't generally think about Nell much except when he was eating at the restaurant. With a flash of insight, he realized that maybe other people didn't either.

"I guess you're right."

A little devil alighted on Jenny's shoulder. "Do you really order the same thing for lunch every time?"

Mason's frown made it hard for her to restrain a laugh. "Yeah, so what?"

"Oh, nothing. I was just curious."

But the tone of her voice told Mason that there was more to it than that. "Curious? What's that supposed to mean?"

"Well, it's just that I was expecting someone who lives out here in the untamed wilds of Montana to be a little less... predictable."

Mason's mouth almost dropped open. *She thinks I'm predictable?* "Are you saying I'm boring?"

"No, not at all. Well, perhaps I shouldn't say that because I don't know you very well. You could be boring enough to put a saint to sleep for all I know," Jenny responded.

Mason stared at her for a long moment before he saw a smile tug at her mouth. When she raised her eyes to his, they glittered with humor. A grin spread over his face as he laughed and shook a finger at her. "I can see I'm gonna have to keep my eye on you."

Her cheeks pinkened a bit when she smiled. "I'm afraid I don't know what you mean, Mr. Crawford."

Mason chuckled. "Please, call me Mason."

"Very well. And you may call me Jenny, on one condition."

"Which is?"

"When Nell comes back, tell her you changed your mind and you'd like something different."

Mason shook his head. "Why?"

"Because it would show both me and her that you aren't boring."

Gazing into Jenny's lovely blue eyes, Mason found himself agreeing to her request. The last thing he wanted was for her to think she was marrying a man who couldn't hold her attention. It was a little unsettling how quickly he'd gone from dreading her arrival to being eager to please her.

When Nell returned with Jenny's lunch, he asked if it would be all right if he ordered something else. Instead of her getting angry as he'd expected, Nell's face lit up and she rattled off something that Mason would never have ordered for himself. Then, before he'd been able to answer, Nell had hurried back to the kitchen, her skirt swishing behind her.

Turning to Jenny, who had an impish grin on her face, Mason wondered if he was about to marry a sorceress instead of a schoolteacher.

CHAPTER 3

*A*lthough it was hot, there was a pleasant breeze that Jenny enjoyed as they drove to the Crawford ranch. The farther they got from town, the wilder the countryside became, but she didn't mind. There was a different quality to the vibrant blue sky here. It almost seemed to sparkle as the sun shone down on them.

Back in Ohio, she'd lived in Cincinnati, and there were times when the tall buildings there made it hard to see the sky. The air quality there wasn't always good, because of the factories, but here in Montana, there was plenty of fresh air. They drove past a large field that stretched for miles to the horizon, and Jenny felt something relax in her soul.

"Tomorrow, I'll show you around town, but I thought you'd like to get settled and rest up some before supper."

Jenny turned her attention to Mason and stifled a yawn.

Her belly full of the excellent food Nell had served her and her eyes full of the pleasant surroundings, she did indeed feel sleepy. Taking a nap was a very welcome idea. "I must confess that I am rather tired."

"I'm not surprised. I won't let my folks keep you too long. Plenty of time to get more acquainted over supper," Mason said.

"I appreciate that. I don't mean to be disrespectful, and I'm looking very forward to meeting your aunt and uncle, but I'd like to be able to stay awake and enjoy their company."

Mason gave her an understanding smile. "You'll need to be fresh for that. Aunt Cecilia will talk your ear off."

Jenny couldn't resist teasing him. "Maybe she'll tell me some stories about your childhood."

Mason groaned. "She loves doing that, and always tells the most embarrassing ones."

"I'll ask her about those right away, then," Jenny responded.

As they neared the turnoff for the ranch, Mason thought that Jenny wasn't like any schoolteacher he'd ever met. She was funny and beautiful and not in the least shy. He'd been afraid that she'd be on the boring side or too shy to talk much. It was a relief to find out that wasn't the case.

"Wait until I'm out of the house first, all right?" he requested. "Spare me a little embarrassment."

"I'll think about it."

Mason smiled at her cheeky response.

He slowed the horse and turned to the right, leading them along the lane that led up to the house.

As they went up the gradual incline, Jenny saw a large farmhouse come into view. It was an attractive structure, with blue shutters that contrasted nicely with the white wooden siding. A long porch that ran the length of the front of the building was shaded by maple trees. There were a few rocking chairs with wicker seats placed on it, and Jenny imagined that it was the perfect place to sit and keep cool in the summer. Soon, they pulled up to the home, which had a welcoming feel about it.

Mason jumped down from the buggy, jogged around to her side, and held out his hand. Again, Jenny felt a spark of attraction as she slipped her hand into his and let him help her to the ground. No sooner had they started for the front door when it was thrown open and a rather tall, lanky woman wearing a green calico skirt and white blouse stepped onto the porch. Over her skirt, she wore a gray calico apron upon which she wiped her hands, and Jenny surmised that she must have been working in the kitchen.

An older man followed the woman down the porch steps. Both had welcoming smiles on their faces, and Mason introduced Jenny to them right away.

Cecilia held out a hand to Jenny. "My, but you're a pretty thing. Isn't she, Mason?"

Jenny blushed, but the pink that crept up Mason's neck was amusing.

"Yes, Aunt Cecilia, she sure is," he said.

Jenny blushed deeper when she saw a genuine appreciation in his eyes. "Thank you," she murmured.

Linking arms with her, Cecilia urged Jenny toward the house. "Now, come on with me. Mason and Herb can bring your trunks. I put you in the guest room next to our bedroom. It gets plenty of shade and gets cool at night. You'll sleep like a babe."

"I appreciate your thoughtfulness," Jenny said, meeting Cecilia's dark eyes.

"You're welcome. I'll show it to you, and you can have a lie-down," Celia said. "You must be exhausted."

Jenny smiled. "I won't lie and tell you I'm not."

"Have you eaten?"

"Oh, yes. Mason treated me to a very nice lunch as soon as I arrived."

Cecilia nodded approvingly. "Good. I was going to scold him if he hadn't."

Jenny liked Cecilia's friendliness and her motherly attitude toward Mason. She'd been nervous about how she'd be received, but her fears appeared unfounded. "He was the perfect gentleman, I assure you."

"I'm glad to hear it."

Cecilia led Jenny through the front door and right up the flight of wooden stairs that started from the small foyer.

Various pictures hung on the floral wallpapered wall on the right side and a white banister with spindles ran up half of the staircase. Jenny was too tired to give the photographs more than a cursory glance as she followed Cecilia.

Upon reaching the upstairs hallway, Mason's aunt turned right and went to a room at the very end of the corridor.

"Here we are," she said, opening the natural pine door and gesturing for Jenny to go in first.

Entering the room, Jenny felt the temperature drop a few degrees, bearing out Cecilia's remarks that it was the coolest bedroom. Pretty, rose-pattern curtains fluttered in the breeze coming through the two windows, and a single bed with a colorful patchwork quilt was situated between them.

Small oval braided rugs covered the floor on either side of the bed. A nightstand sat to the right of the bed and a small cushioned chair took up the opposite corner. The last piece of furniture in the room was a long, intricately carved bureau with a large mirror.

"This is a lovely room," Jenny said.

Cecilia smiled at the compliment. "Thank you."

Boots sounded on the stairs and, soon, they were joined by the men. The women stepped back as Mason and Herb lugged Jenny's trunks into the room and stacked them against an empty wall. Mason had laid her carpetbag on top of her trunk and he handed it to her.

"Thank you both for bringing them upstairs for me," Jenny said.

Herb smiled. "Sure thing. Well, me and Mason got work to do."

"That's right, but I'll see you at supper," Mason agreed.

Cecilia moved toward the door. "The bathroom is right next door. Let me know if you need anything. I'll be in the kitchen."

Jenny thanked her as the trio left and closed the door. Alone, she looked around the room. Her gaze settled on the bed and she felt exhaustion tug at her. She gathered a few things from her carpetbag and went to the bathroom. There was fresh water in the dry sink and a few clean washcloths hung nearby.

Jenny washed her face and neck and took down her hair. She brushed it out and drew it back in a low ponytail with a ribbon. She completed the rest of her toilet and went back to her room. Undressing down to her chemise, she pulled down the quilt and slipped under the cool linen sheet. The stress of her long trip had taken more of a toll on her than she'd realized and, in no time at all, she sank into slumber.

"She sure is a looker, son."

Mason smiled as he pounded a strand of barbed wire fast to a fence post. "I won't argue with you there. Her picture was pretty enough, but she's even more so in person."

Herb stretched out the next section of wire and held it in

place against a fence post. "Does that mean you're glad we pushed you to get a bride?"

Mason shot him an annoyed glance but nodded. "Yeah."

Herb laughed. "Don't sound so unhappy about it. You know we only want what's best for you."

"Don't get me wrong, but I'd have liked to pick a wife in my own time."

"You did pick Jenny in your own time," Herb countered.

Mason straightened and wiped sweat from his brow with a forearm. "How do you figure that?"

"Well, we got you to start writing women, but you didn't choose the first woman you wrote to," Herb replied. "It was a couple of months before you got Jenny's letter, and you seemed taken with it almost right away."

Mason pointed his hammer at Herb. "No. Aunt Cecilia was taken with it, not me."

"That's a load of hogwash, Mason. You forget how well we know you. When you told us about Jenny's letter, you had that excited look you always get when something interests you."

Mason couldn't deny that, but he'd still felt pressured about the whole affair. However, there was no use stewing over it. Jenny was here, and he was looking forward to getting to know her. "Well, that's all water under the bridge. I'm just looking to the future." He grinned. "I must say that it does seem pretty bright."

Herb chuckled, and they returned to their work. When

the sun started sinking in the sky, they collected their tools, left the west pasture, and headed for the big red barn situated a little up the road from the house. As they walked along, Mason wondered if Jenny had had a good rest. The image of her curled up on a bed popped into his mind and his pulse ran a little faster.

He succeeded in halting that train of thought while they fed the stock for the night, but he found himself hurrying through his chores, eager to see Jenny again.

JENNY WOKE with a start when someone tapped on her door.

"Supper will be ready in just a little, Jenny," Cecilia called.

"Very well. I'll be down soon," Jenny responded.

As Cecilia's footsteps retreated down the hall, Jenny stretched and yawned. Looking out the window, she saw that the sun was inching toward the horizon above a distant mountain. It was cooler in the room and Jenny felt refreshed. The savory scent of meat tantalized her nose and her stomach felt empty, as though she hadn't eaten lunch just a few hours ago.

Rising, Jenny opened her top trunk and found a fresh dress. It was made of lilac linen and had a bit of lace at the collar. It was lightweight and would keep her cool, which she was sure she would appreciate as it was sure to be warm in the kitchen. She put on a simple white corset over her chemise and then donned the dress.

Stepping over to the mirror, she made sure that the dress was neat. Her hair was another matter. She ran a brush through the curly mass, plaited it, and wound the long braid into a bun at the nape of her neck, which she pinned in place. After applying a little rose water behind her ears, Jenny was ready to go downstairs.

She opened her bedroom door and was surprised to encounter Mason, who was just coming out of the bathroom.

"Evenin'," he said.

The way his gaze swept over her made Jenny feel warm, and she returned the favor. He'd washed up, but a light stubble shadowed his jaw, giving him a more rugged appearance that stirred her female senses.

"Evening," she said.

"Did you rest good?"

Jenny lifted an eyebrow. "Yes, I rested *well*."

Mason caught the way she'd stressed the word and smiled. "I can see I'm gonna have to learn to speak a little better around you."

"What kind of schoolteacher would I be if I didn't correct your grammar a little?" Jenny inquired. "I promise not to become annoying about it, though."

"Good to know." Mason nodded toward the stairs. "We best get moving or Aunt Cecilia will come looking for us."

"Well, we wouldn't want that." Jenny walked past him

and her stomach fluttered a little at his nearness. "Whatever she's cooking smells wonderful."

Mason followed her and Jenny felt his eyes on her the whole way down the stairs.

"To the left," he said as they reached the first floor.

Jenny walked through the doorway into a large kitchen. Green checkered gingham curtains hung at the windows and cheerful rag rugs were placed in front of the back door, under the big round table and chairs, and in front of the sink with a pump. She hadn't expected them to have such a modern convenience, and it was a pleasant surprise.

Herb had been sitting at the table, but he stood and smiled upon seeing her. "There she is. Looks like your nap agreed with you, Miss Carson, judging by those bright eyes of yours."

Jenny chuckled. "Yes, it certainly did. Please, won't you all call me Jenny?"

"Very well, Jenny," Herb said.

"Is there anything I can do to help?" Jenny asked Cecilia.

The older woman waved her toward the table. "No, no. You sit down and relax. I'm just finishing up."

"Please, I insist," Jenny said.

After considering for a few moments, Cecilia said, "All right. You can put the biscuits and butter on the table."

Helping with the meal made Jenny feel less like a guest. She also didn't want any of them to think her lazy, least of all Mason. It wouldn't do to have her future husband think he was marrying a woman who was useless around the house.

Once everything was ready, they sat at the table. Herb said a simple blessing and Cecilia started passing dishes to everyone.

"How many children were you a governess to?" Cecilia asked.

Jenny smiled at the fond memories of the Harper children. "Just two. They're twins. Eloise and Edward. They were so mischievous, but such a delight, too."

"Why did you quit?" Herb asked around a bite of pot roast.

"Stop talking with your mouth full," his wife scolded him.

Herb's gray eyes crinkled as he laughed. "See what you two have to look forward to."

Jenny's eyes met Mason's. His mouth twitched in amusement, and she couldn't hold back a giggle. Soon they were all laughing, and Jenny felt even more comfortable with Mason's family than she already had.

When their mirth subsided, Herb repeated his question, without food in his mouth.

Jenny replied, "I didn't quit. Mr. Harper owns a couple of shipping companies and other business ventures. He moved their family to England for at least two years while he works on a merger and learns the other company's business. Governess positions in Cincinnati are scarce and highly sought after, so I was unable to find employment with another family."

Cecilia put more potatoes on her plate. "Is that what made you want to be a mail-order bride?"

Jenny had been dreading this question, but she wouldn't lie. "Honestly, it was my brother Eli's idea. Well, more like a dare."

Mason's brows drew together. "Your brother dared you to become a mail-order bride?"

"No, not exactly." Jenny searched for a way to explain it to them. "Eli and I have always been very close and very competitive. We made a bet with each other and we came up with outrageous things that the other would have to do if they lost.

"Eli decided that if I lost, I would have to answer a mail-order bride advertisement. He'd seen the advertisement for an agency in the newspaper and thought that it would be funny. If he lost, he had to call on one of the neighbor girls and take her for supper at least once."

Mason stopped chewing and put his fork down. "So, you lost the bet and wrote to me?"

Jenny's heart lurched at the anger brewing in his eyes. "No, I mean, yes… I lost the bet, but that's not why I wrote to you."

"I'm confused," he said.

"You're not the first gentleman I wrote to."

"I'm not? How many did you write to?"

"Four." Jenny knew she was bungling this, but she couldn't figure out how to make it better. "I wrote to the first gentleman as a bet, but I never heard back from him. I hadn't thought seriously about marriage until then, but it made me wonder if it wasn't time.

"There were a few men I'd seen at parties or church, but none of them had ever interested me much. You'll think me fanciful, but I found something romantic about finding a husband by exchanging letters. Some things are easier to discuss in a letter than in person."

Mason wasn't sure what to think. He didn't like the idea of his search for a bride being treated like a joke. On the other hand, he'd only started looking because of Herb and Cecilia's prodding, which he imagined would upset some women. "You said you wrote to a few other fellas before me. What made my advertisement different?"

His question gave her the perfect opportunity to explain it all. "I liked your honesty. You weren't promising all sorts of unrealistic things or using a lot of flowery language to explain what you wanted in a wife. It was simplistic and to the point."

Cecilia asked, "What did the advertisement say? He would never tell us, and he wouldn't let me write it for him."

Her nosiness annoyed Mason, but he figured that it couldn't harm anything to tell them now. But Jenny beat him to the punch.

"I still have the advertisement and all his letters. Mason, may I read it to them?"

Although he was a little bashful about it, Mason decided that it would be easier than trying to remember exactly what it had said. "I guess that'd be fine."

Her smile mesmerized him, and he wondered what was wrong with him. He'd never considered himself the kind of man whose head was turned by a pretty face, but there was something about Jenny that addled his brain a little.

"Thank you. I'll do that after dinner," she said.

Her excitement about it reassured Mason that she was happy about coming to Montana and, once again, he was taken aback by how much that mattered to him. As they continued eating, he made up his mind not to resist it. After all, wasn't it better to enjoy being with the woman he married instead of spending the rest of his days with a wife he couldn't stand? He was grateful that Jenny had picked his advertisement and sent a prayer of thanks heavenward.

CHAPTER 4

*A*n hour later, the four of them sat out on the front porch, enjoying some coffee and shoofly pie that Cecilia had made earlier that day.

Jenny pulled a folded piece of newspaper out of her dress pocket and moved a little further into the light from the lantern that hung overhead. "Are you sure you are happy for me to read this to them, Mason?"

Mason swallowed a bite of pie. "Sure. I'm curious about it myself because I don't quite remember what it said."

Jenny opened the clipping and read, "*Twenty-nine-year-old rancher in the Montana Territory seeks marriage-minded woman.*"

Mason smiled. "I sorta copied that beginning from a few others I saw. I never looked at them before, so I didn't know how it worked."

"Well, I think it's commendable that you took the initiative to find out," Jenny commented before continuing. "*My folks raised me to respect women, and I'll be a good husband. I can provide for a family, and some people say I'm not bad to look at. I'll be happy to send a picture if I get one in return. We don't have servants or the like, so it's best if you can cook and keep a house. Knowing how to sew wouldn't be unwelcome since I work with a lot of fencing and I'm always tearing my shirts.*"

Cecilia let out a snort of laughter. "Don't I know it? It seems like I'm repairing a shirt or replacing buttons every week. I never saw a man so hard on clothes."

Herb laughed. "That's because he's a hard worker and he's not afraid to get his hands dirty."

Jenny tried not to blush as she thought about the pleasant way Mason's rough palm had felt against hers, but she wasn't sure she was successful. She read on to distract herself. "*One last thing; the woman I marry must like to dance. I look forward to receiving letters of interest and promise to reply back.*" Jenny smiled. "Your whole advertisement was very nice, but those last two lines were the ones that really captured my attention."

"Why's that?" Mason asked.

"Because they showed that you like to have fun, and that you are a man of your word. Those things are very important to a woman," Jenny answered.

Cecilia said, "Truer words were never spoken. A man

doesn't have to be the most handsome man to be attractive to a woman. If he can show her a good time and make her laugh when she's unhappy and he's honest, kind, and principled, that's what matters most to a woman."

Jenny sent a sidelong glance Mason's way. "I can see that Mason is all those things, but I will say that it doesn't hurt that he's also quite handsome."

Mason couldn't control the way his chest puffed out at her compliment. "Thank you. It doesn't hurt that you're pretty as spring flowers."

Jenny blushed, which made Herb chuckle.

"It does my heart good to see you two getting on so good," he said right before he yawned. "Well, that's my cue to go to bed. Tomorrow comes early."

Cecilia joined him when he rose. "Yes. We'll let you two have a little privacy, but don't be up too late." She pointed at Mason. "Behave yourself."

Mason mentally rolled his eyes, but said, "Yes, ma'am."

"Goodnight, and thank you for such a warm welcome," Jenny said.

"You're welcome, dear. Goodnight."

VOICES WOKE Jenny early the next morning. She lay in bed and smiled as she thought about the previous night. She and Mason had talked for almost an hour after his aunt and uncle had gone to bed. He'd told her about some of the towns-people and explained a few things about the ranch. She'd enjoyed his funny stories about the trouble he and two of his friends used to get into. It had been easy to picture a young Mason playing jokes on his classmates or sneaking off to fish.

Mason had also asked her about her family and forma-tive years. She'd appreciated the way he'd paid attention to her. It had been clear that he was genuinely interested in her. He hadn't been bored by their conversation and, more importantly, he hadn't found her tedious or annoying.

Jenny jumped when someone knocked on her door. "Yes?" she called out.

"Good morning," Mason answered. "Aunt Cecilia drew you a bath downstairs."

The sound of his voice made Jenny smile. She got out of bed and put on her robe. "A bath sounds wonderful. Please thank her for me."

"Of course. Uh, did you sleep well?"

Jenny suppressed a giggle as she moved closer to the door. "Like a baby. Thank you for asking."

"Sure thing. Well, I'm off to do the milking, but I'll see you at breakfast."

"See you later."

When Jenny heard him walk down the hall, she hurried to gather a few toiletry items, then opened the door. She felt a little apprehensive about walking through the house in only her nightclothes and robe, but she was covered and the men weren't there, so she continued downstairs to the kitchen.

"Good morning," she greeted Cecilia, who stood at the sink.

Cecilia turned around and smiled at her. "I'm jealous."

Jenny's brows jumped up. "I'm sorry?"

"It's not every woman who looks that pretty first thing in the morning."

Jenny ran a hand through her hair as she laughed. It was a little mussed, but she was glad that it wasn't sticking up all over. Cecilia led her into a little room off the kitchen where there were a chamber pot and a decent-sized metal bathtub. Steam rose from the hot water inside the tub. White linen curtains provided privacy but allowed light to enter the room, even though they were closed. A small chair stood next to a narrow table in the corner but, otherwise, the room was empty.

"I'll leave you to it," Cecilia said before closing the door.

Jenny hung her robe and nightclothes on a peg on the back of the door and stepped into the tub. She sank into the water and sighed. It had been over two weeks since she'd had a proper bath and it felt incredible.

She allowed herself to soak for several minutes before starting to wash off the travel dust and sweat. Remembering that Mason was showing her around town that day, she wasted no further time in finishing up. Once she was in her nightclothes and robe again, she brushed out her hair and left the bathing room.

The kitchen was empty, so she went upstairs, making a mental note to ask where she should empty the bathwater when she came down. She didn't expect Cecilia to wait on her. Once in her room, she donned a dark green skirt over several petticoats. She didn't wear as many underskirts as usual because she'd noticed that Cecilia's skirt wasn't as full, probably because she did a lot of housework and farm chores.

Once she was dressed, she brushed her hair again and pulled it back, tying it at the nape of her neck with a piece of green ribbon so it would be out of her face while it dried. Descending the stairs, she entered the kitchen just as Cecilia came in the door carrying a basket.

"Got quite a few eggs this morning. I'm surprised the hens are laying so good in this heat," Cecilia told her.

Jenny resisted the urge to correct Cecilia's grammar. "That's good news."

"That's right. If nothing else, we'll always have eggs to eat."

Jenny smiled in response. "Where is your bathwater emptied? I'll get rid of it. I insist on looking after myself, so please don't treat me as a guest."

Cecilia nodded approvingly. "Very well." She had Jenny follow her into the bathing room. "There's a trough right outside this window and we just scoop the water out into it.

There's a hole in the bottom of the trough and underneath that is a French drain. It lets the water drain away slowly and doesn't harm anything."

"A French drain?" Jenny asked as Cecilia opened the window.

"I don't understand it all, but Herb said that it was used in olden times to drain water away from places, so he thought making one here would be easier than carting the water outside and dumping it somewhere," Cecilia replied.

When Cecilia moved away from the window to get the bucket that sat under the table in the room, Jenny poked her head out the window. The wooden trough was empty at the moment, allowing her to see the hole in the bottom. Looking to her left, she saw a long line of rocks, about as big as large potatoes, running away from the house.

"That's ingenious," she remarked. "Not only does it get rid of the dirty water, but it keeps it from damaging the foundations of the house."

"That's right. Does 'ingenious' mean smart?"

Jenny withdrew from the window and smiled. "Yes. I'm sorry. I don't mean to sound like a know-it-all."

Cecilia wagged a finger at her. "Never be sorry for being smart."

"Yes, ma'am."

"That's better. You empty that, and I'll get breakfast started. Those men will be back soon, and they'll be as hungry as a couple of bears."

Jenny smiled and got on with the task at hand.

MASON WAS GREETED by several people as they entered town, but he didn't stop to chat. He planned to introduce Jenny to everyone, but he wanted to get to the schoolhouse that doubled as the church when Pastor Gibbons was in town. Paul Gibbons liked to take care of his clerical business in the morning before going to visit shut-ins, and Mason wanted to catch him before he left.

He explained his reasoning to Jenny; he didn't want her to think he was being antisocial or trying to slight her. He was relieved that she was understanding and agreed that this was the best course of action.

Arriving at the schoolhouse, Mason helped Jenny out of the wagon. He'd brought the wagon because he needed to get some staples that wouldn't fit in the buggy. Jenny took a few moments to look the schoolhouse over. The clapboard structure wasn't large, but it looked sturdy and there were three windows on the side facing her. She assumed there were three on the opposite side as well.

A shiny brass bell hung in a small belfry on the roof, indicating that it was new. Various shrubs and flowers had been planted around the outside and four wooden steps led up to the front door. Along with the door, all the windows were open to let the cool morning breeze in. Excitement filled Jenny's breast as they walked to the stairs. This was where she'd start her career as a schoolteacher, and she couldn't wait to begin.

Jenny mounted the stairs and blinked in the dimmer lighting of the cloakroom where children would hang their winter coats and cloaks and store their lunch buckets. Her eyes adjusted as they went through the cloakroom into the schoolroom, and she saw a middle-aged man with dark eyes look up and smile from behind a desk.

"Ah, Mason!" The man stood and walked toward them. "It's good to see you again."

Mason said, "Likewise, Pastor Gibbons."

He introduced the clergyman and Jenny to each other.

"So, this is your bride-to-be. Word travels fast in small towns like this," Paul said in response to Jenny and Mason's surprised expressions.

"Yeah, that's right," Mason said. "We came to see when you'd be able to marry us before you leave."

Paul beamed at them. "I have exciting news! I was going to wait until the town meeting to announce this, but I won't be leaving. I'm starting a permanent church here in Spruce Valley!"

"How wonderful!" Jenny exclaimed. "Congratulations. I'm sure everyone will be thrilled."

"I certainly am," Paul said. "I'd also like to congratulate you on taking over as our schoolteacher. I hope you won't mind continuing to share the building until the church is built."

"Not at all," Jenny assured him.

Paul gave her a slight bow. "You are as gracious as you are pretty."

Jenny chuckled. "And you are a flatterer."

"Perhaps, but it's true. Don't worry, Mason, I won't try to steal her away," Paul said with a wink.

Mason grinned. "Glad to hear it. I'd have to fight you if you did."

"Now, now, gentlemen," Jenny chided them. "No fighting in the church."

"Right you are." Paul pulled out his pocket watch from his suit vest pocket. "My, look at the time. I must go, but we'll talk soon about the wedding."

Mason said, "How about you come to supper tonight, Pastor? The folks would be glad to see you, and you'd get a home-cooked meal."

Jenny thought she detected a note of urgency in Mason's voice, but she didn't remark on it.

"How can I refuse such a generous offer? I hate to rush off, but we'll catch up this evening. A pleasure to meet you, Miss Carson."

Jenny gave him a small curtsy. "Good day, Pastor Gibbons."

Paul gave them a parting smile and hurried from the

building. A few moments later, they heard hoofbeats fade away. Jenny started inspecting the schoolhouse. Five rows of oak double-desks were separated by a center aisle that led up to the teacher's desk, which sat in front of a large blackboard.

Windows were situated on either side of the blackboard. In front of each window stood a long, short bookcase that was filled with books. Turning around, Jenny saw that each of the double-desks had two slates sitting upright, which meant that each child would have their own slate, assuming that there weren't too many pupils.

A black pot-bellied stove stood in the righthand corner at the back of the room. A floor-to-ceiling wooden cabinet took up the rear left-hand corner. Jenny surmised that it must contain supplies. Going to inspect the teacher's desk, Jenny noticed a small lectern off to the side that must be used by Pastor Gibbons during Sunday services.

She sat down in the wooden chair. It had a burgundy cushion on the seat and castors that made moving around on it easy. The desk wasn't huge, but it would be more than adequate for what she needed. It had a center drawer and three more down the right side. A cup of pencils, an inkwell, and the attendance ledger sat on the desktop along with a kerosene lamp. On a small table next to the desk, a globe stood proudly.

"What do you think?" Mason asked.

She rose and looked around the room. "It's a lovely

school, and it will be an honor to teach the children here. It has everything I need and more."

Mason's shoulders sagged a little with relief. It was important to him that she approved of the way the school was set up. "Glad to hear that. I'm the chairman of the town council, so just let me know if there's anything you need and I'll pass it on to the rest."

Jenny's chin rose and she gave him a direct stare. "Did your last teacher sit on the council?"

Mason's mouth thinned for a few moments. He saw where she was going with this, but he wasn't sure how to approach it. "Yes, he did, but…"

Jenny arched her right eyebrow. "But I'm not welcomed on the council since I'm a woman, correct?"

These subjects with women were always tricky for Mason. He wasn't prone to lying, so he couldn't deny what she'd said, but he also didn't want her feelings to be hurt. Something occurred to him. "We've never had a woman in an important position like this before, so I don't rightly know."

Jenny stepped closer to him and his pulse rose a little as her rosewater scent tantalized his nose. "Do you personally disapprove of women holding important positions?"

Another tricky question. "Um, well, I wouldn't say 'disapprove,' but…" The way her eyes narrowed just a fraction made him hesitate. "I'd have to say it depends on the woman and the situation."

Although she'd been prepared to argue, Jenny couldn't find fault with his response. It was true that not every woman would be suited to sitting on the town council and, since Mason didn't know her, he wouldn't know whether she was capable of the task. If she were honest, she wasn't sure she was qualified, either, since she'd never done such a thing.

"I agree, and since I've never been a schoolteacher before, I think it's best if I concentrate on running a school first before I get lofty ideas about being elected to council," Jenny said.

Mason held back a sigh of relief. "That's probably wise, but that doesn't mean you can't tell me your ideas. I ain't taught school before, so I don't know much about it."

"You *haven't* taught school," Jenny said.

Mason chuckled at her correction. "No, I *haven't*."

"You catch on fast, Mr. Crawford," Jenny said.

He moved a little closer. "Does that mean I'm the teacher's pet?"

Jenny couldn't think for a moment. Her eyes lowered to his mouth for just a second, but the way his eyes darkened said that he'd noticed it. A slow smile curved his lips, further addling her brain.

She regained her composure and looked at him through her lashes. "I didn't plan on having a teacher's pet. But in your case, I might make an exception."

Mason took another step. "What do I get if I'm a good student?"

"Perhaps a few pieces of candy."

Mason considered that for all of two seconds. "I was thinking of something a lot more exciting and even sweeter."

Never had Jenny considered herself the kind of woman to be affected by a man so much, but then she'd never met a man like Mason before. "And what would that something be?"

"I'd rather just show you."

Voices from outside cut through the spell he'd woven around her, but she didn't want him to think she wasn't interested. "I might let you do that… In a more private place."

They heard footsteps ascending the steps. Mason stepped back, but he sent Jenny a smile that made the room feel almost sweltering.

Three children ran through the door; two young boys and a little girl.

"You're our new schoolteacher!" the tow-headed girl said as she ran up to Jenny. "You're pretty."

"Well, thank you." Jenny chuckled. "Yes, I'm Miss Carson. What's your name?"

"I'm Betty and these here are Ethan and Lenny. Them's my brothers."

Jenny ignored Betty's bad grammar. There would be time enough for instruction once school began. "It's so nice to meet you all."

The oldest boy scowled. "I can't come to school. Pa needs me at home too much."

"You can come, Ethan," Betty protested. "At least sometimes."

"You don't know anything. You're too little to understand," Ethan said. "We ain't rich like *some* people and can't hire hands to help. I'm all Pa's got." He shot a look of animosity at Mason.

The other boy, who seemed a couple of years younger, spoke up. "I can help at home, too."

Ethan put a hand on the younger boy's shoulder. "You know you can't do the heavy stuff yet, Len. Best you get some learnin' while you grow."

Lenny fell silent, but his expression sank gloomily.

"How old are you all?" Jenny asked.

"I'm seven. Ethan is twelve, and Lenny is ten," Betty replied.

"I see," Jenny said. "Your sister is right, Ethan. You could come a couple days each week and you could also work with Lenny on his lessons."

Ethan fixed her with a stubborn look. "I don't mean no disrespect, ma'am, but I ain't comin' to school, and that's that. C'mon, you guys. We gotta get our stuff at the store and get back home."

Betty stuck her bottom lip out. "But I want to…"

"Now, Betty," Ethan said. "There's too much to do at home to stand around jawin'."

Betty stuck her tongue out at him but took the hand he held out to her. "Bye, Miss Carter," she said, giving Jenny a jaunty little wave as Ethan pulled her along. Lenny looked down at the floor as he followed his siblings out the door.

Jenny smiled to herself over Betty's mispronunciation of her name. When Mason let out a heavy sigh, she turned to him. "What's wrong?"

"I worry about those kids," he said. "Their father, Andy Franklin, is about as pleasant as a cornered raccoon. Our families have never gotten along. His parents passed up our land and bought another piece of property because they thought it was better for farming since there weren't a lot of trees on it."

Jenny said, "I take it that the land wasn't ideal."

"You'd be right. Turned out that it was rocky ground and most of the good topsoil had been eroded by some heavy spring storms." Mason walked over to one of the windows. From there, he could see the Franklin kids as they walked down the path that led to the main street.

"My parents, Uncle Herb, and Aunt Cecilia went together and bought our ranch, which borders the Franklin land. The land had a lot of trees, which was one of the things they liked most about it. Clearing it wasn't a problem since they needed the lumber for building the house and barn and fencing.

"Plus, there was plenty of firewood. But Pa and Uncle Herb were smart about the way they cut the trees down.

They did it right as planting season began and planted as much grass as possible. Ma and Aunt Cecilia put in a big garden and, by harvest time, we had more produce than we needed and enough hay and straw to get us through the winter."

Jenny came to stand beside them. "So, they've been jealous of your family all these years?"

"Yeah. Once they saw how fertile our land is, they accused us of stealing it from them. They tried to get us in trouble over it. But we didn't do anything wrong, so the circuit judge tossed the case out after less than five minutes," Mason said. "But that's not all they hate us for."

Jenny grew even more concerned. "What do you mean?"

"As I told you in my letters, Grandpa and Grandma were the first people who settled around here."

"I remember," Jenny said.

"Well, when more people started making their homes here, everyone decided to name the town after them. The Franklins wanted to name it something else, but they were way outnumbered."

Jenny shook her head. "They sound like very unpleasant people, who unfairly blame people for their own misfortune."

"Yeah, well, they don't see it that way. And judging by the way Ethan acted with me, it seems like Andy's been passing that hate down to them," Mason said.

The regret in Mason's eyes made Jenny feel sorry for

him. He was clearly a caring man, and she wished that things were different between the two families.

Mason shook off his dark musings. "But that's enough of that. Are you about finished up here?"

Jenny took a last look around, her excitement returning. "Yes. It seems as though everything is in order."

"Looks like it," Mason agreed, smiling at the happy light in her eyes. "Let's go pick up our supplies and I'll introduce you to everyone. Folks have been mighty curious about you, so be prepared for lots of questions."

"I assure you that I'm up for the challenge."

Mason could believe that about her. Even though he'd only known her for a day, it was clear that Jenny could handle herself in social situations. As they left the school-house, he knew that she'd have the citizens of their little town eating out of the palm of her hand in no time.

CHAPTER 5

*S*itting at the dinner table with Mason's family that night, Jenny held a hand to her aching stomach. It turned out that Pastor Gibbons had a great sense of humor and liked telling amusing stories about his years as a clergyman. His current story was about the worst fruitcake he'd ever been given.

"The generous soul who made it was well-intentioned, and I couldn't refuse her gift. However, once I bit into it, I could barely open my mouth because it was as strong as any glue created. It took quite a while to get it down. I'm afraid that it was inedible, but I didn't want to throw it out and waste it." His warm chuckle made Jenny smile. "At the time, my wife Annette and I had a couple of pigs. We ended up giving the cake to them. They must've thought it was delicious because they gobbled it up in minutes."

Laughter filled the room when he finished his tale. When it subsided, Cecilia and Jenny went to get dessert for everyone.

As they plated up the cherry crumb pie Cecilia had made that afternoon, she said, "It's wonderful that Pastor Gibbons will be here permanently now. We'll make a donation toward building a new church, and we have plenty of trees at the edge of the western pasture that would make nice boards."

Jenny was starting to learn her way around the kitchen. She put a pot of coffee on the stove and took some cups out of the cupboard. "I'm sure he'll be very grateful to you for your kindness."

"It's the least we can do. Everyone will benefit from having him in Spruce Valley." Cecilia sent a sly glance Jenny's way. "It also means that he'll be available to marry you and Mason whenever you'd like."

Something between excitement and fear made Jenny's stomach drop, but she forced a bright smile. "Yes, that's right. Mason and I haven't had a chance to discuss our exact plans yet."

Cecilia chuckled as she filled a creamer and put it alongside a sugar bowl on a tray with the dessert plates. "I'd be surprised if you had since you've only just gotten here. I'm just joshing you, but I'll be happy to help you with anything you need."

"That's so kind of you, but I may ask you for so much help that you'll regret your offer," Jenny said.

"No, I won't. Herb and I were never blessed with children, so we doted on Mason. But I've always wanted a daughter," Cecilia said. "So, having you around will sort of feel like I have one."

Her sentiment brought sudden tears to Jenny's eyes. "I can't tell you how much that means to me."

Cecilia patted her shoulder. "No need to. Well, let's get this out to those men before they come looking for us."

Since her mother was so far away, it comforted Jenny to have someone like Cecilia to rely on. That Cecilia was Mason's aunt, and that she approved of her, made Jenny feel even better. With a warm glow inside, Jenny wiped away a tear and helped take the dessert to the dining room.

HEAT LIGHTNING FLICKERED several miles away from the Crawford farm as Jenny sat on the porch later that night. She'd helped Cecilia clean up after dinner while the men had talked in the parlor. Pastor Gibbons had left about an hour ago, and Mason and Herb had gone to the barn to check on the stock for the night. As she looked out over the lawn and listened to the crickets, Jenny felt a sense of contentment.

Although she'd been worried that things would go wrong once she'd reached Montana, her concerns seemed to be unfounded. The Crawfords were a good family and Mason was a good man. *Easy on the eyes, too*, Jenny thought with a smile.

"You look happy."

Jenny startled at Mason's voice, making her chair rock a little. "I swear you're like a cat!" she scolded.

Mason laughed and lowered himself into the chair next to her. "Sorry. I wasn't trying to sneak up on you."

He briefly touched her hand, and Jenny's pulse jumped.

"You had such a pretty smile on your face. What were you thinking about?"

Jenny was glad he couldn't see the blush his compliment brought to her cheeks. "All sorts of things. How pretty it is here, how excited I am about teaching…"

"Anything about me?"

"I had maybe one or two thoughts," she teased.

"And what were these couple of thoughts?"

"That you eat enough for three men and have a nasty habit of scaring people."

Mason laughed at her witty remark. "I only eat so much because I work hard every day. What's your excuse?"

Jenny gasped and promptly pinched his forearm. "Cooking and serving a meal is certainly work, Mason! Besides, your aunt's cooking is delicious, so who could blame me for taking a second helping?"

Mason's laughter made her giggle. "Boy, it sure is easy to get you riled up." He placed his hand on her forearm. "But I like spirited women."

"Do you? And just how many spirited women have you known?" she asked, trying to ignore the heat that seemed to be spreading up her arm.

Mason understood exactly what she was asking him. "I've courted a few girls, but it wasn't anything serious. A couple of them were pretty spunky."

Jenny had no right to be jealous of these other women, but a little green-eyed monster seemed to dance around her. "Did you love any of them?"

"They were all nice enough. But no, I never fell in love with them."

Trying to sound nonchalant, Jenny asked, "How well did you know them?"

"A couple of them grew up around here, so pretty well. The others had moved here, but they found husbands and they moved away." He leaned a little closer to her. "But if you're asking whether I knew them in the biblical sense, the answer is no."

Jenny turned to look at him. His eyes were a lighter shade of silver in the moonlight and his hair moved slightly in the lazy breeze. His broad shoulders and strong arms filled his shirt out in a way that made it hard to look away. Mason was the kind of man who drew female eyes without even trying.

It was impertinent, even rude of her to ask, but she needed to know. "Have you ever known any woman in the biblical sense?"

Mason wasn't offended. He liked her courage and, even though it was a little embarrassing, he smiled. "No, I haven't. I came close a couple of times, but I got myself reined in before things went that far."

His answer surprised Jenny. She'd been expecting him to either refuse to answer her or to tell her that he'd slept with at least one woman. He was so handsome that it was hard to believe that he hadn't a slew of women chasing him.

"I'm glad," she blurted. "I mean, that is… Why? Never mind. It's none of my business." Jenny was embarrassed for being so nosey about something so personal.

"It's all right," Mason said, wanting to make her feel better. "Since we're getting married, we should know everything about each other, even the stuff that's hard to talk about." He took her hand. "I didn't go past a certain point with a woman for several reasons. First, I'd never want to have a child out of wedlock, and I didn't want to have a shotgun wedding."

Jenny liked the feel of his strong hand around hers. "I can certainly understand that. That's one reason I've resisted that temptation. The other is that I was waiting for marriage."

Mason would've still married Jenny if she hadn't been a virgin, but knowing she'd never been with a man made him happy. "I feel the same way, and I'm glad you do, too."

He stroked his thumb across the back of her hand and Jenny almost shivered from the contact. It amazed her that a man she'd just met could have such a strong effect on her. She squeezed his hand back and smiled.

Their gazes locked and she couldn't look away, mesmerized by the heat in his eyes. Instinctively, she knew he wanted to kiss her, and she wanted the same thing. Growing bold, she leaned a little closer and tipped her face up to his in a clear invitation.

Mason's blood ran hotter as he looked down at her. She was so beautiful and smelled so good. His hunger was stirred too much to resist her offer. Lowering his head, he brushed his mouth against hers. When she didn't pull away, he brought his hand up to cup the back of her head as he deepened the kiss.

Never had he kissed such soft, sweet lips. She tasted of cherry and coffee, a heady combination. She moaned against his mouth, fisted a hand in his shirt, and pulled him closer. Mason had never had such a swift reaction from a woman before, but he wasn't complaining.

With his free hand, he pulled her chair against his and wrapped his arm around her. His ardor rose higher and he plundered her mouth with urgency. If she'd signaled him to stop, he would've immediately heeded her request, but she seemed as lost as he was.

The feel of his arm around her and his firm chest under her hand assaulted Jenny's senses in a most delicious way. He smelled of hay and horses, two scents she'd never thought she'd like on a man. But Mason wasn't just any man. He was confident and strong, yet kind and thoughtful, and so gorgeous that it was sometimes hard for her not to stare at him. She ran her hand up his chest, marveling at the way his muscles flexed under her palms.

The chair arm cut into her ribcage, making her grunt in pain. She drew back, breaking the kiss. Her rapid breathing was echoed by Mason's as she stared into his eyes. "I'm sorry. The chair was hurting me."

Concern joined passion in his gaze. "Are you all right?"

"Yes. I'm fine, just disappointed that it interrupted us," she replied.

Caressing her cheek, Mason struggled to regain control, but Jenny had brought out something primal in him. "Maybe it's best that it did. I didn't mean to get so carried away."

Jenny leaned back in her chair, grateful for the breeze that helped cool her heated cheeks. "Yes, I think you're right. Goodness, Mason."

Mason chuckled. "I agree. It's improper to say this, but judging by that kiss, I don't think it'll be too long before youngins come along."

Pressing her fingers to her lips, Jenny tried to contain the giggle that rose in her throat, but it was hopeless. "Agreed," she choked out before lapsing into laughter.

Mason's hand closed around hers and he laughed with her. After a few moments, she sobered. "I believe it's time for me to retire for the evening."

"Not just yet," Mason said. "How do you feel about getting married on Saturday?"

Jenny's breath hitched. That was only four days away. However, she already had her dress and the ceremony wouldn't be lavish, so planning it wouldn't take much time. Cecilia and Herb would be their witnesses. She'd saved as much of her governess wages as possible for the trip West, and she had plenty to cover a nice dinner at the Station to celebrate after the service.

Gazing into Mason's eyes, Jenny asked herself if she was ready to marry him. It was a serious decision; once they'd said their vows, there'd be no going back. Happiness stole into her heart and the answer it sent back was a resounding yes.

"I would love nothing more than to become your wife on Saturday."

The grin that spread across Mason's face sent her heartbeat skipping along. "I'm glad to hear it. We'll tell Pastor Gibbons right away."

Excitement overtook Jenny, and she squeezed his hand. "Yes. Right away. Now, I really must go before I throw myself at you again."

Mason laughed. "Feel free to throw yourself at me anytime."

Jenny stood and wagged a finger at him. "No, no. That's enough for now."

Mischief shone in her eyes as she bent down and pressed

her lips to his. Before he could capture her, she danced away, gave him a flirtatious little wave, and went inside.

Mason wondered how he'd gone from dreading marriage to being anxious to tie the knot in only a couple of days. He was a practical man by nature, and not given to flights of fancy. But there was something about Jenny that made him forget common sense. Instead of being dismayed over it, Mason felt lighter, happier than he'd been in a long time.

When he'd been a young man, his mother had told him to choose his future bride wisely. She'd said that while it was important to be sensible about picking a wife, it was much better to find a love match.

Mason wasn't sure about love, but he liked Jenny an awful lot and she was the most beautiful woman he'd ever laid eyes on. Wasn't he supposed to admire and desire the woman he was going to spend the rest of his life with? He smiled as he imagined his parents approving of his aunt and uncle's insistence that he get married. Something deep in his soul told him that he'd chosen the right woman. Saturday couldn't come soon enough.

CHAPTER 6

*O*ver the next few days, Jenny began settling into her new home. Always thirsty for knowledge, she eagerly soaked up information about all things related to running the ranch. Since she'd never done that kind of work before, she paid close attention to Cecilia's instructions on gathering eggs, milking cows, and cooking.

It surprised her how much of the manual labor fell to women. Cecilia did everything from throwing down hay for the milk cows to carpentry work when something minor broke. She also did all the usual women's work such as sewing, mending, cooking, and cleaning. Jenny didn't know where the older woman got all her energy.

When she commented on it, Cecilia said, "It's different for women out here. Lots of times, the men are working far from the house or away on cattle drives, so we have to fend for ourselves. We have to be able to move the steers to different pastures, mend things when they break, and keep the place going. If we have heavier work that we just can't do, sometimes we ask our closest neighbor fellas to help, but there's no guarantee they have time. So, we have to find ways to do it."

Jenny's appreciation for pioneer women had grown even greater after this explanation, and she became determined to become as proficient as possible at ranching life. Her curiosity about the work extended to the business and financial side of the operation. At first, she'd been hesitant to broach the subject with Mason. But she thought that, since she'd have to help with all the manual work when the men were busy or out of town, she'd also need to be familiar with their finances.

One night after supper, she and Mason took a walk, enjoying the cooler night air, and she took the opportunity to bring it up.

"Mason, do you think I'm intelligent?"

He gave her a sidelong glance as they strolled up the lane toward the main road. "Of course I do. Otherwise, we wouldn't have hired you as the schoolteacher."

She nodded. "In that case, I'd like to learn more about our finances and how to run our ranch." Mason grinned and chuckled, making Jenny bristle. "Are you making fun of me?" she demanded.

His eyes widened and he raised a calming hand. "No, I'm not. I just like hearing you call it *our* ranch, that's all."

Jenny's irritation faded and she smiled. "Oh, I see. I'm sorry for being so touchy, but where I come from, women are often treated as delicate creatures with no minds of our own. We're good enough to marry, have children with, and so on, but it's rare for women to be allowed an education beyond a certain point. I was fortunate to have a father who thought that women's minds are just as capable of higher learning as men's."

One of the herd dogs had accompanied them. Mason found a stick on the side of the road and threw it for the dog before answering. "As you've seen, Aunt Cecilia is a strong, smart woman. If she wasn't, our ranch wouldn't be doing as well as it is. You also know that women here work just as hard as men.

"I've noticed the way you pitched in and started learning right away. Aunt Cecilia says you're a quick study and that you haven't complained once. It's a relief that you're so capable and willing to do farm work. It's also good that you want to learn the business. So, I don't mind teaching you about it at all."

Relief and pride filled Jenny. "I'm so happy that both of you approve of me."

Mason stopped walking and turned to face her. "It ain't just us. Uncle Herb and the ranch hands do, too."

"They do?"

"Yeah. They've also noticed how pretty you are." His smile captivated her. "I had to make it clear that I wouldn't tolerate any inappropriate behavior toward you."

A blush tinged Jenny's cheeks as she chuckled. "Well, women aren't averse to a little admiration. As long as it goes no further than that, I don't mind either."

Mason's expression sobered, and an intense light lit his eyes in the deepening twilight. "Well, I do, and I let them know it."

"Goodness, Mason," Jenny said. "I didn't know you were so possessive."

"I never was before I met you." He closed the distance between them and slipped an arm around her waist. "I can't stand the thought of another man putting his hands on you." He pulled her against him. "Or anyone else kissing you."

Jenny's heartbeat accelerated as Mason glanced at her mouth before meeting her gaze. She answered the question in his eyes by tilting her face up to his. He captured her lips, igniting her passion. She responded in kind, reveling in the warmth of his lips and how good it felt to be in his arms.

Her mind reeled when Mason broke the kiss. "Dang, Jenny. I can hardly control myself around you."

Jenny giggled and laid her head against his chest. "The feeling is mutual. You didn't hear me complain, did you?"

His laugh rumbled under her ear. "No. But that doesn't help any."

Laughter overtook Jenny and Mason joined in as he drew

away. He took her hand and tugged on it. "I think we best go back to the house before I get carried away again."

Jenny sent him a saucy smile. "I don't want to, but I suppose it's prudent. Although, I will say that I don't mind getting carried away with you."

Mason groaned. "You are a wicked woman, Jenny. I swear you've cast a spell on me."

She nudged his arm. "Perhaps I have. How do you feel about me getting a black cat?"

Their laughter filled the night as they teased one another on the way back to the house, and Jenny felt happier than she could ever remember.

THE NEXT DAY, as Jenny and Cecilia worked in the large vegetable garden, Mason rode by on his way to the barn. He smiled and waved. Jenny returned his greeting and watched as he rode out of sight. Jenny loved the natural way he sat a horse with his back and broad shoulders straight yet relaxed. Despite the strength in his work-roughened hands, he had a light touch on the reins.

Cecilia's chuckle interrupted Jenny's daydreaming about her handsome man. She blushed and smiled sheepishly.

Cecilia's eyes gleamed with humor and a knowing smile tugged at her lips. "There's nothing to be ashamed of, dear.

Mason's a good-looking young man, so I'm not surprised that you'd look at him like that."

"Yes, Mason is quite attractive," Jenny said. "I'd be lying if I said I didn't find him appealing. He's also a good man, no doubt due to his excellent upbringing."

Cecilia gave a short laugh. "We've done our best to raise him right. I'm glad our lessons stuck with him and that he's following our example. He was a little rambunctious when he was younger, but that's normal for boys. But he settled down, and we're proud of the man he's become."

Jenny bent down to pull a few weeds that were growing close to a tomato plant. "He's never spoken of his parents. I don't mean to pry, but I can't help being curious about them."

Cecilia straightened, threw some weeds in the bucket they'd brought with them, and wiped her hands on her apron. "Well, it's a sad story."

Jenny moved down the row a little. "I'll understand if you'd rather not tell me. I know how painful losing loved ones is. My father passed away from consumption a few years ago. So, I'm acquainted with that kind of heartache."

Cecilia's gaze turned sympathetic. "I'm sorry for your loss."

"Thank you."

Gazing off to the field beyond the garden, Cecilia said, "Hank and Rose were the most wonderful people. She was a little too serious sometimes, but Hank could always pull a laugh out of her. They were so devoted to each other. Mason looks like his ma. She was so pretty. Hank was tall and lanky like Herb, and he had dark eyes that always seemed to have a smile in them."

Jenny smiled at the picture of Mason's parents that was being painted.

Sadness tinged Cecilia's expression. "Mason was only nine when they passed." She gestured toward the field. "Their house was just over there. Hank was always a stickler for keeping the chimney clean, so we're not sure how it caught fire one night while they were all asleep. One of the ranch hands got up to go to the outhouse and saw the flames.

"He alerted everyone and started throwing buckets of water on it while Herb ran in the house to get everyone out." Cecilia swallowed before continuing. "Hank and Rose had inhaled a lot of smoke and they were already gone. They brought them out, but we couldn't revive them. Mason was farther away from the chimney, so he didn't inhale as much smoke. He coughed a lot that day, but he was fine otherwise."

Tears sprang to Jenny's eyes as the horrible scene rose in her mind. It was awful enough to lose a parent, but doubly so to lose both in such a terrible manner. "I can't imagine how devastating that must have been. Mason told me that they'd passed away, but he didn't tell me how it happened."

Cecilia brushed away a couple of tears. "He doesn't talk about it much. He was withdrawn and angry for over a year after it happened. We tore down the house, but we also had to completely remove the foundations because it upset him so much whenever he looked at it."

"That's understandable," Jenny said. "I would have felt the same way. I wish I could've met his parents."

Cecilia smiled and put a hand on Jenny's shoulder. "They'd have liked you. You're just the sort of woman they would've wanted for Mason."

"Are you sure?"

"Positive."

A warm glow spread through Jenny at the thought that Mason's parents would have approved of her. The subject was dropped then, and the women returned to their work. As she pulled weeds and removed dead leaves from various plants, Jenny's mind turned to her future husband, and she grew even more eager for their wedding day to arrive.

CHAPTER 7

*W*hen dawn came on Saturday, a misty rain was falling, but it didn't dampen Jenny's spirits at all. Her excitement about marrying Mason outweighed any nervousness she felt. She hummed as she bathed, imagining the wonderful life ahead with an equally wonderful man. Her initial impression of Mason had been confirmed over the last four days.

Everyone she'd met had only had good things to say about him and his family. He'd taken her on a couple of outings as well. One night, he'd surprised her with a picnic supper. On another, they'd gone to the Station for dinner. He was always attentive and amusing, and he treated her with respect.

They'd shared several passionate moments, but he'd never tried to go beyond a certain point. Jenny had kissed other men, but none had ever incited such passion in her. When she'd come to Spruce Valley, she hadn't expected to be so attracted to her future husband, and she was glad that they got on so well.

She took great care as she dressed in a mint green satin dress with a tight bodice and puffy sleeves. She wore enough petticoats to make the full skirt flare out, which gave it an elegant swish when she moved. Cecilia helped braid several sections of her hair and create an intricate updo.

Her mother had given her small emerald earrings, handed down from her grandmother. She put them on and looked at herself in the mirror. The earrings complimented her dress and drew attention to her graceful neck, and Jenny was satisfied with her appearance.

"You're a vision, Jenny," Cecilia said, coming to stand beside her. "Mason won't know what hit him when he sees you."

Jenny smoothed her skirt. "Are you sure I look presentable?"

"As sure as I'm standing here."

Jenny took Cecilia's hands. "Thank you for all your kindness and for helping me get ready today. Since my mother can't be here, you're filling her shoes and I couldn't be more grateful."

Cecilia blinked away tears as she hugged Jenny. "I'm glad to do it, and I'm so happy you're joining our family. Mason's getting himself a fine woman."

Jenny returned the embrace for several moments before drawing back and brushing away tears of her own. "Thank you." She looked at the clock on her bureau. "Goodness! We must leave or we'll be late. I don't want to keep Mason waiting."

"You're right. I'll tell Herb to bring the buggy over to the house."

As Cecilia left the room, Jenny took a last look at herself in the mirror. It would be the last time she did so a single woman. Thinking about the wonderful future ahead of her, she turned from the mirror and followed Cecilia.

MASON STOOD at the front of the schoolroom, looking at the clean blackboard. His lips twitched as he contemplated writing: "Welcome to the wedding of Mr. Mason Crawford and Miss Jenevieve Carson." A couple of nights ago, she'd informed him that Jenny was her nickname and that her mother had chosen an unusual spelling of Genevieve to be unique.

Since Jenny wasn't an uncommon name, he'd just assumed that it was a shortened version of Jennifer. He realized there were a lot of things he didn't know about Jenny, but they had the rest of their lives to get to know each other. His stomach tightened with anxiety as the reality fully hit him. He was about to become a married man, to tie himself to a woman for the rest of his life.

"You doing well, son?"

Mason turned around to face Paul. "Yeah. Just thinking."

Paul smiled at him. "I'm sure you're a little nervous, but there's no need to be. Jenny is a fine woman, and you're a lucky man to have found someone like her."

"I know. I just hope I'm a good husband to her. Can I tell you something?"

Paul looked toward the doors. None of the guests had shown up yet, so he said, "Yes, of course. Go ahead."

Mason blew out a breath and straightened his suit jacket. "I didn't want to get married. I only advertised for a mail-order bride because Aunt Cecilia and Uncle Herb coaxed me into it. Well, sort of forced my hand. I know they were only doing what they thought was best for me, but I resented them for it."

Paul grew concerned. "Do you still feel that way?"

Thinking about Jenny, Mason smiled. "No. When I first went to meet Jenny, I felt like I was being led to the gallows. But as soon as I met her, that changed. I don't know what I expected, but it sure wasn't such a beautiful, smart, fun lady like her."

"I'm very relieved to hear that, Mason. I've married couples before who were getting married for the wrong reasons," Paul said. "It's not something I care to repeat, especially in your case. Are you ready to marry her?"

Mason placed a hand over his heart. "I know this will sound crazy because I haven't known her long, but I think I'm falling in love with her." This was hard for him to say. It made him feel vulnerable and scared, but he couldn't deny what his heart was telling him. "She makes me happy and I can't imagine my life without her now. Yes, I want to marry her."

Paul's dark eyes glittered with happiness. "That's wonderful! We never know when the Good Lord will send us our partner, but when it happens, we should embrace it. Your folks knew what they were doing. Perhaps God urged them to prod you about it. I'm confident that you and Jenny are a good match, and that you'll be very happy together."

Paul's confirmation of his own feelings bolstered Mason, and he felt better for having talked to the pastor about the situation. "Thanks, Paul. I appreciate that."

"You're quite welcome," the pastor replied.

Shortly after, people started filing into the schoolhouse that was being used as the church for the day. The school desks had been pushed against the walls, and benches had been brought in for the guests to sit on. Mason smiled as he imagined how surprised Jenny would be to see them. He'd been surprised about it when Damon had informed him on the sly that the townspeople had sort of invited themselves, stating that they refused to let the wedding of the town founders' grandson take place without celebrating the occasion.

Damon's wife, Maggie, approached him with a big smile on her face. "Well, there's the groom. You look quite dashing, Mason."

Mason returned her warm hug and kissed her cheek. "Thanks, Maggie. It's so good to see you. Thanks for coming."

"Of course, I'd come," she said, releasing him. "Nothing would keep me away from your wedding. I'm so happy for you. Jenny's a lovely girl." She pointed at him. "You'd better be good to her, or you'll be sorry."

Mason chuckled. "I promise that I'll treat her right."

"Glad to hear it."

Damon joined them. "I imagine you got a little case of the jitters."

"Well, I did, but I think that's passed now," Mason admitted. "I can't wait until she gets here."

"I'm sure you won't have to wait long," Maggie said. "Let's go get a seat while we can, Damon. It's going to get awfully crowded." She patted Mason's arm. "All will be well."

Mason smiled as they left him and his eyes strayed to the window, looking for any sign of his bride-to-be.

"Now, now," Paul admonished. "No peeking."

Grinning, Mason said, "Can you blame me?"

"Of course not, but you must exercise a little patience, Mason." The pastor's smile took any sting out of his words.

Mason smiled back. "Yes, sir." He resisted looking out the window after that, but it wasn't easy.

As THEY ARRIVED at the church, Jenny's previous confidence slipped a little, but she kept her nervousness to herself. She closed her eyes for a moment and said a quick prayer, imploring God to calm her nerves and let her focus on the happiness of the day.

She reopened her eyes and noticed that several buggies lined the right side of the church, which had the most shade. "Is there another ceremony today?" she asked.

This was often the case, especially when a community had a circuit preacher who was only in town on certain days. Word might not have spread that Pastor Gibbons was now Spruce Valley's permanent minister.

Cecilia turned in the front seat, an impish smile on her face. "They're all here to watch you and Mason get married. Damon told Herb yesterday that a lot of folks decided to come."

Jenny's eyes widened. "But I haven't invited anyone. Did Mason?"

Herb laughed. "No, but around here, we don't always wait for an invitation. We all just assume we're invited to things like this since we're such a small town."

"What about a reception?" Jenny asked, starting to feel

panicked. "I haven't planned anything, haven't had time to plan one since we were getting married so soon."

Cecilia replied, "Don't worry about that. It's all taken care of."

Jenny thought about her limited funds. "I don't have enough money to pay for a big affair."

Herb pulled the horse to a halt and got out. "No one expects any money, Jenny. They'll have brought plenty of food with them, and Damon and Maggie are hosting it at the Station. They're doing it because they care about Mason. And they like you, too. Now, stop worrying and just enjoy the day."

"Listen to him," Cecilia chimed in. "I married a smart fella."

Jenny trusted her future in-laws, and if they said she shouldn't worry, then she wouldn't. Besides, there was nothing she could do about it now. Herb helped her out of the buggy and Cecilia helped her fix her dress.

When she was done, she gave Jenny a last critical look over. "There. All set."

"I'll go let them know you're here," Herb said as they came to the bottom of the schoolhouse steps. "Wait right here."

Cecilia looped her arm through Jenny's and gave it a squeeze. "Nothing to be nervous about, child. You'll see."

Bolstered by Cecilia's support, Jenny's previous anticipation returned, and she grew impatient to see her groom.

Herb returned and offered his arm to Jenny. "I know I can't really take your pa's place, but I'd be right proud to give you away."

Tears stung Jenny's eyes as she thought about her deceased father. She'd always imagined him giving her away, but she was touched by Herb's kindness. She took his arm and smiled up at him. "I'm most grateful to you, and I'd be honored for you to give me away."

Cecilia kissed her cheek. "I'll see you inside," she said and headed up the steps.

Jenny took a deep breath and said, "I'm ready when you are, Herb."

Herb lifted his chin and squared his shoulders. "Well, then. Let's go get you hitched."

Jenny smiled as he helped her up the stairs. They stepped into the cloakroom and stopped for a few moments.

Herb asked, "Ready?"

Jenny gave him a firm nod. "Ready."

CHAPTER 8

*W*hen Jenny appeared in the doorway on Herb's arm, a warm feeling spread through Mason. She looked exquisite in her green gown and emeralds glittering at her earlobes. He'd never seen a more beautiful sight. Mason wanted to take her in his arms and tell her so. It was hard to control himself and stay in place as Herb escorted her down the aisle to him.

Although her smile was a trifle hesitant, her sapphire eyes sparkled. Transfixed by her beauty, everyone else faded away and Mason felt like they were the only two people in the world.

Herb smiled at Mason as he reached the front of the schoolroom. He handed Jenny over to him. "I know you'll be good to her, son." He clapped Mason's shoulder, kissed Jenny's cheek, and went to sit with Cecilia.

Holding Jenny's hands, Mason whispered, "You're the most beautiful thing I've ever seen."

Jenny squeezed his hands back. "And you're the most handsome man in the world."

She meant it. His fine black suit fit him to perfection, and he looked so different, so extraordinary. Meeting his eyes, she saw desire sparkling in their silvery depths and felt an answering hunger. She squelched it when Pastor Gibbons started the ceremony, reminding herself that there would be time for that later.

As the pastor guided them through the ceremony, they both recited their vows with sincerity, pledging to honor and cherish each other for the rest of their lives. Neither could look away from the other, and something between them solidified when Mason slid a gold band on Jenny's ring finger.

"I now pronounce you man and wife," Paul said. "You may kiss your bride."

Jenny went into Mason's arms eagerly, a thrill running through her when he pressed his lips firmly to hers. It was a short kiss, but it still kindled a fire in her, and when he released her, she was a little out of breath. Mason's expression mirrored the way she felt.

Paul presented them to the congregation and applause filled the building. Jenny couldn't stop smiling as she and Mason made their way down the aisle to the door. He led her outside and down the steps, where they stopped to wait to greet the guests as they left.

Jenny admired the way her ring looked in the sunlight, and it seemed unbelievable that she was now married to the man at her side.

"Do you like it?" he asked.

Smiling, Jenny said, "I love it. It's beautiful."

Seeing the ring on Jenny's finger made Mason proud that she was his now, and he vowed to always be worthy of her. "I'm glad."

"Did you know all these people were coming?" she asked.

Mason laughed. "Not until Damon told me when I got up this morning." He'd stayed in one of the rooms over the mercantile last night so that he wouldn't accidentally see Jenny before the wedding. "I sure was surprised."

"So was I," Jenny said. "It's so kind of the Frosts to host the reception in their restaurant."

"They have two of the biggest hearts I've ever known," Mason said.

Herb and Cecilia came outside and descended the steps. They embraced Mason and Jenny and stood beside them as the other guests began exiting the schoolhouse. The Crawford family was greeted and congratulated by around fifty people, many of whom Jenny was meeting for the first time.

Jenny felt so touched that they'd attended, but she knew

that it was because they were friends with Mason's family. She hoped that she would get to know them before long; she wanted to continue making friends and to get to know her pupil's families. Watching the interaction between the townspeople and Mason, it was evident to Jenny that he was very popular.

Their admiration for him didn't seem tied to the fact that he was part of the town's founding family. The informal way they joked and spoke with him was genuine. Jenny joined in the conversation, expressing her gratitude for them coming to the wedding and for the reception that would soon follow. She was warmly met, and it made her heart glad to be accepted.

When the last well-wisher had left them, Mason offered her his arm. "I don't know about you, but my belly is as empty as a saloon beer barrel on a Friday night."

Jenny and Herb burst into laughter while Cecilia scolded him for his crude remark. Mason pretended to be sheepish, but he winked at Jenny as they walked toward the mercantile. As they approached the eatery, the sound of many voices reached their ears, and when they entered the Station, it was filled with people who were putting the finishing touches to the meal.

Nell guided them over to a table at the head of the room that was decorated with a lacy white tablecloth. A pretty floral centerpiece and china dishes kept company together on it. She urged them to sit and then hurried away.

Pastor Gibbons called for silence so he could say the

blessing, and everyone bowed their heads. When he was finished, Nell escorted the happy couple to the food tables to fill their plates first.

"I still can't believe the change in Nell," Mason whispered to Jenny as they returned to their table. "You certainly have a way with people."

"Well, I just pay attention, that's all." She gave him a teasing look. "Men don't always do that as well as women."

Mason seated her and sat down beside her. Giving her a wicked grin, he said, "I pay attention when you're around. I can hardly think about anything else when you're in sight."

Jenny blushed as she giggled and took a sip of her cold lemonade.

Mason chuckled but relented as he turned to his food. His statement about being hungry hadn't been made in jest. He'd been too nervous to eat breakfast, but his appetite had returned in full force. Tucking into his meal, he tried not to think ahead to their wedding night too much, but it was difficult to keep it from his mind whenever he spoke with Jenny.

Her pretty pink lips were so tempting to him and it was hard to resist kissing her. The way she glanced at his mouth every so often didn't help, and he started wishing away the time until they could start their honeymoon. Then he told himself that there was no rush, that they'd only have one reception and he wanted to enjoy every minute of it.

Jenny enjoyed the succulent chicken and tasty side dishes immensely and she planned to ask for the recipes of her favorites so she could make them for her family. She was a fair cook, but she wanted to become as skilled as Cecilia in the kitchen. She didn't think it was fair to leave all the cooking to the older woman but realized that they hadn't discussed the running of the household yet.

Her thoughts were interrupted by the strains of a fiddle. On the right side of the room, four men had set up chairs and started warming up their instruments. Two of them played fiddles, one played spoons, and the other had propped a washboard on his knee.

When they struck up a waltz, Mason rose and held out his hand to her. "I believe it's customary for the bride and groom to start off the dancing, Mrs. Crawford."

Jenny's heart fluttered at the sound of her married name and the thought of dancing with Mason. She didn't hesitate to take his hand. She loved to dance, and it had been a while since she'd had the chance. Since governesses looked after the children while their parents attended parties and outings, she hadn't had many opportunities for entertainment.

Mason got a kick out of the way she pulled him to the area that had been set up as a dance floor. "Something tells me that you're a good dancer," he commented as he took up the proper stance.

"You're correct, Mr. Crawford."

"Thought so. Well, I might be a rancher, but Ma and Pa were good dancers and they taught me. I won't embarrass you."

Jenny smiled up at him. "As long as you don't step on my feet, I'm not worried about your dancing abilities."

"I can do a lot more than keep off your toes."

Mason began moving, his steps graceful and confident. Jenny delighted in the way he guided her around the floor and she lost herself in the dance. They seemed to move together as one, as though their minds were connected.

Mason had danced with his share of women, but holding Jenny as they swayed and turned was his most enjoyable dancing experience. He was transfixed by her sparkling eyes and beautiful smile. He'd do almost anything to make her happy, just to see that expression on her face.

When the dance ended, the band started a fast jig. Mason taught Jenny the steps and they laughed together at her mistakes, but she was quick to catch on and was soon performing the dance well. They spent the next couple of hours dancing and conversing, and it was a magical time for the newlyweds.

Several women invited Jenny for tea, or to join their quilting circles. Their offers of friendship meant the world to her, and she looked forward to spending time with them. She also talked to them about their children and the upcoming school year. By the time the reception wound down, Jenny had a tentative total of eighteen children who would attend her school classes.

After a few people left, Mason decided that it was time for him and Jenny to also depart and begin their honeymoon.

Herb and Cecilia were going to stay with family for a few days to give the young couple some privacy. They made the rounds, thanking everyone for giving them such a special day, then went to their buggy.

Assisting Jenny into it, Mason asked, "Ready to go home, Mrs. Crawford?"

Jenny's smile made his heart beat a little faster. "More than ready, Mr. Crawford."

Mason climbed into the buggy and started their horse out. Once they'd left the town behind, Jenny moved closer to him, and his stomach tightened at the tantalizing scent of her perfume. The graceful curve of her neck and smooth, pale skin of her shoulders drew his gaze, and he wanted to taste her skin.

With effort, he pulled his gaze away and focused on the road ahead, but he urged their horse into a faster trot, anxious to get his new bride home.

THE SUN STREAMING through the windows the next morning woke Jenny. She stretched and the memory of the previous night returned to her. Opening her eyes, she found herself in Mason's bed – their bed now – and blushed as she remembered the passion they'd shared. Since both of them had been virgins, their lovemaking had been awkward and shy at first, but it hadn't taken long for instinct to take over.

Jenny shivered as she remembered the ecstasy Mason had given her, and she looked over at his side of the bed. She frowned and rose up on her elbow upon seeing that it was empty. Her frown turned into a smile when she saw the small dressing table that Mason had given her as a wedding present. Her silver brush and mirror sat on its surface, along with her jewelry box and other items.

Looking around the room as she rose from the bed, Jenny decided that Mason's room needed a woman's touch. It was a nice room, with a large walnut bed and furniture, but the rust-colored curtains weren't to her liking. A nice blue pair would be better as they'd brighten the room. She'd just donned a sheer silk robe over her satin, low-cut nightgown when Mason entered the bedroom.

He stopped still upon seeing her. She looked gorgeous. Desire sent hot blood surging through his veins as he set the breakfast tray he carried on the bureau. The pleasure they'd shared a few hours ago was fresh in his mind, and his body responded.

He tried to ignore it as he smiled at her. "Good morning, beautiful. Um, how do you feel?"

The concern in his sheepish expression touched her. "I feel wonderful. How are you?"

A lazy grin curved his mouth, and she felt a powerful urge to kiss him.

"I'm pretty wonderful myself." He gestured at the tray.

"I wanted to surprise you with breakfast in bed, but you're already up."

"It smells great. I'm famished. We can still enjoy it right here." Jenny sat on the bed and patted the space next to her.

Mason scooted the dressing table stool over beside the bed, set the tray on it, and sat beside Jenny. "I'm not as good a cook as Aunt Cecilia, but I do all right."

Looking over the spread of scrambled eggs, salt pork, and fried potatoes, Jenny's stomach seemed even more empty. He'd also brought a carafe of coffee and tiny bowls with sugar and cream. "Goodness. I didn't know you were so talented in the kitchen."

Mason chuckled as he started fixing her a plate. "I don't know about talented, but my food is passable. Aunt Cecilia has taught me some things over the years."

They enjoyed a leisurely breakfast, discussing a myriad of subjects and laughing at each other's jokes. Mason was taking a couple of days off to spend with his new wife and the ranch hands had been instructed not to disturb the couple unless absolutely necessary.

"Thank you for the tasty breakfast," Jenny said when they'd finished eating.

"You're welcome."

Mason moved the tray to the bureau and returned the stool to its rightful location. Turning back to Jenny, he froze at the intense way she was staring at him. Need ignited inside him as he saw desire shimmer in her eyes. Returning to the bed, he sat beside her and slid an arm around her waist. It was as though she'd been made to fit against his body.

She wound her arms around his neck and tilted her face up to his. "How do you feel about going back to bed?"

Mason's wicked grin showed his approval of the idea. As they set sail again in a sensual sea, Jenny fervently wished that the tempest of passion would never end.

CHAPTER 9

A month passed, four weeks that were the happiest of Jenny's life. From the way he doted on her to the way he made love to her, Mason was a constant source of joy. Although he sometimes worked long days, they made the most of their evenings together. Some nights, Cecilia and Herb retired early to give them privacy.

School had been in session for two weeks, and Jenny loved her job. The wide age range of her students didn't daunt her at all. In fact, she enjoyed the mix of ages and the differences in how their minds worked. There were several good students, and two that were exceptional. Jenny asked them to help some of the younger students with spelling and arithmetic while she worked with the older students who were struggling.

At the end of every school day, Jenny was mostly satisfied with her students' progress, but she always strived to teach them just as well the next day. Although it was important to her that she make a good impression on the townspeople, educating their youngsters mattered much more to her.

Their well-being was always foremost in her mind, which was why she always took extra food with her. Several ranch kids often had no more than a lard sandwich for lunch. Jenny couldn't stand the thought of children going hungry and made sure they had something good to eat so they could concentrate on their lessons instead of an empty tummy.

One morning near the end of September, Lenny Franklin arrived at school with a bruise on his right cheek. When she inquired about it, Lenny mumbled that he'd had an accident in the barn. His little sister, Betty, had been a little withdrawn for the rest of the day, but Jenny just thought that she was worried about her brother.

However, as the days went by, Lenny had a couple more poorly explained bruises, and the Franklin children's behavior changed. Betty, who'd been bubbly and amusing, was now quiet and, toward the end of the day, she often grew restless. Finally, Jenny questioned Lenny and Betty in private to see if there was something amiss, but they insisted that all was well. Their denial rang hollow, and she had the feeling that there must be trouble at home.

As she drove the buggy home that afternoon, she

couldn't get the children off her mind, and she was distracted during supper.

"Jenny, is everything well?"

Mason's question broke through her musings. "Oh, yes. I'm fine."

"What's on your mind?" His silver eyes were filled with concern.

"I'm very worried about the Franklin children," she replied.

"Why?"

Jenny's appetite left her as Lenny's haunted expression rose in her mind. "Something isn't right at home."

Mason arched an eyebrow. "What makes you say that?"

Gathering her thoughts, Jenny told the rest of her family what had been occurring with Lenny and Betty.

Herb put his silverware down. "What exactly do you think is happening?"

Jenny replied, "I believe that there might be some abuse occurring."

Mason's eyebrows jumped higher. "That's a pretty big accusation, Jenny."

"I know, but it's the only thing that accounts for Lenny's injuries and the changes in his and Betty's personalities," Jenny said. "And Betty always seems to dread the end of the school day, as though she doesn't want to go home."

Cecilia laid a calming hand on Jenny's forearm. "I'm

sure things are fine, but it's good that you're watching out for them."

"That's right," Herb said. "Keep an eye on them, though."

"Yes, I will." Jenny let the matter drop, but she was convinced that she was right.

Later that night, she sat on the porch with Mason, watching the stars.

Mason watched the play of moonlight on her face and knew he'd never tire of looking at her. "Honey, will you do me a favor?"

Jenny looked at him. "Of course. What is it?"

"I don't want you to do anything about the Franklin kids on your own. If you're still concerned, we'll talk to Sheriff Ryder," he said. "This has to be handled carefully."

"I'm aware of that, Mason, and I would never accuse someone without proof, but I know what I've seen."

The thought of any child being hurt twisted Mason's stomach, but there was a lot at stake. "I'm just saying that with you being married to me, and since Andy hates us... Well, this type of thing could go sideways real quick. It's best to let the proper people handle it."

Jenny reined in her temper but spoke with confidence. "As the schoolteacher, it's perfectly proper for me to deal with this situation. After all, I'm the one who's witnessing it."

Mason placed his hand over hers and squeezed it. "I

know, but promise me that you'll talk to me before you do anything rash."

Knowing that he meant well, Jenny's anger dissipated. "I promise not to rush to judgment, but I won't turn a blind eye to what's happening, either."

Lifting her hand, Mason kissed the back of it. "I'm not asking you to."

A shiver ran through Jenny when his warm lips pressed against her skin. It amazed her that such a small action could stir her desire so much. "Good. Now, let's go to bed."

The seductive look she sent Mason's way said that sleeping wasn't what she had in mind. "I think that's a great idea."

Jenny laughed when Mason rose, tugged her out of her chair, and ushered her inside.

With a supreme effort, Jenny controlled her outrage throughout the school day. Thinking about her conversation with Mason the night before, she decided to talk to Josh Ryder after school was over instead of confronting Andy Franklin on her own.

Ethan had shown up at school with Betty that morning. When Jenny had inquired about Lenny, Ethan had said he was sick, but the way his gaze had slid away from her convinced Jenny that he was lying. She'd known it was pointless to press him further.

The day seemed to crawl by but, finally, the last student left. Jenny quickly gathered her belongings and hurried from the schoolhouse. She responded to people's greetings along the way to the sheriff's office but didn't dawdle. She was relieved to find that Josh Ryder was in when she arrived.

"Hello, Mrs. Crawford. How can I help you?" he asked with an affable smile.

Jenny took a calming breath and began her story. When she'd finished, Josh rubbed his chin and a thoughtful look settled on his face. Jenny tried to curb her impatience while he took several minutes to digest the information she'd imparted.

At length, he said, "Well, I guess I'd better go out there and see what's what. I don't approve of men hitting kids or women. I'll let you know what I find out."

"I'm very grateful to you, Sheriff," Jenny said with a tight smile. "It doesn't matter what time of day or night it is, please let me know how you fare with this."

Josh nodded. "All right. I will."

Jenny expressed her thanks again and bid him a good day. She walked to the mercantile to purchase a few things, feeling a little lighter knowing that the sheriff was on the case.

A SHORT TIME LATER, Jenny was seething with fury as she stood in an aisle of the Frosts' store. She'd been surprised to see Andy Franklin there. Loathing filled her as she listened to the cruel threat he was issuing to Ethan and Betty. He must've accompanied Ethan to pick Betty up.

"Don't ask me for a dang thing," he warned his children. "We ain't got money for extras, so keep your mouth shut if you know what's good for you."

Betty said, "But, Pa, I don't have…"

"I said to keep quiet! We all gotta do without stuff." Andy's voice was a low growl.

"There's no cause to be mean like that, Pa. She's just…"

Betty started to cry. Incensed, Jenny marched around the corner and down the aisle. Andy's back was to her, but he must've heard her approach because he turned around.

Behind him, Ethan stood holding Betty's hand.

"Is everything well?" Jenny asked.

Andy's blue eyes narrowed, and he took a step toward her. "Mind your own business, schoolmarm."

"As the schoolteacher, the welfare of my students *is* my business," Jenny retorted.

Ethan stared at her, shaking his head in a plea to Jenny, but she just couldn't let it drop.

Andy advanced on her again. "You don't know what you're talking about."

Jenny motioned at Betty. "There's no need to be so harsh. She's only a little girl."

Andy's cruel smirk made the hair on the back of Jenny's neck stand on end. "You best leave us alone and keep your nose out of people's business."

"I'll thank you not to threaten me. I don't think my husband would take kindly to that."

Andy's face blanched and then turned beet-red.

Jenny didn't wait for him to respond. She turned and marched away, keeping her spine straight and her head up. However, she shook inside with righteous anger as she got in her buggy and started for home.

"YOU DID *WHAT*?"

Jenny's heart stopped beating for a moment at Mason's harsh tone before it lurched into a fast rhythm. His eyes had darkened to a stormy gray. She'd seen him get angry before, but this was the first time his ire had been directed at her.

"You heard me. Must I repeat it?" Sarcasm tinged her query.

Mason's jaw tensed. "I told you to talk to me first before you did anything."

Jenny was thankful that they were alone in the barn. Mason had been out there when she'd arrived home and he was unhitching her horse. She'd been petting her horse's face, but she walked away as her agitation grew. Horses picked up on emotions and she didn't want to make the mare nervous.

"Why must I talk to you before I speak with the sheriff? I'm perfectly capable of relaying the events of the past few weeks," Jenny said.

Mason freed the horse from the buggy and started undoing the harness. He wasn't used to being annoyed with Jenny, and he didn't like it. However, he felt he was justified. "Okay, I'll give you that you were right in going to Josh, but you shouldn't have confronted Andy on your own."

Clenching her fists, Jenny asked, "What would you have had me do?"

"Go get Damon and let him deal with Andy."

Jenny let out a sarcastic laugh. "Oh, I see. It's fine if a *man* would have confronted him, but not a *woman*. Is that it?"

This was a touchy subject, and Mason knew he had to tread with care. "Yes, but only because I have a feeling that if he got mad enough, he'd have gone after you." He freed the horse from the harness which he then draped over the buggy. He went to Jenny and put his hands on her shoulders. "Jenny, I love you, and it would just kill me to see you get hurt."

Jenny's eyes went wide and her heart beat in triple-time. She knew Mason held great affection for her, but she hadn't known his feelings went beyond that. "You love me?"

Taking her face in his hands, he said, "Yeah. You're everything I could want in a woman and so much more, and I'll be danged if I'm going to let anything happen to you."

Jenny covered his large hands with hers and kissed his right palm as happiness surged through her. "Oh, Mason, I love you, too."

"You do?"

"Yes. I have for a while, but I was afraid to tell you in case you didn't return my feelings," Jenny said.

Mason wrapped his arms around Jenny's waist and pulled her close. He lowered his head and claimed her lips in a fierce kiss, trying to convey all he felt. Her immediate response excited him, but it was short-lived. She broke the kiss and stepped out of his arms.

"This makes me happier than I can tell you, but it doesn't mean that I agree with you," she said. "I appreciate your concern, but I'm a grown woman, and I can take care of myself."

Mason planted his hands on his hips and glowered at her. "God knows I admire your bravery, but you don't have the fighting skills to defend yourself from a mean son of a gun like Andy."

Jenny conceded that point. "I know, which is why I left the store when I did. I'm sure that Josh will successfully deal with Andy. He's going to let me know what happens. So, the problem will be solved."

Mason wasn't convinced. "Josh will do his best, but you

can't change a person with one warning. I want you to stay away from Andy. If you meet him on the street or whatever, just avoid him. If he gives you any trouble, get somewhere safe and send for Josh. Andy's the kind of guy who would want revenge."

Jenny refused to be intimidated. "I won't stop speaking up on any child's behalf."

Mason ran a hand through his hair. "I'm not asking you to. I just want you to be careful."

"You must think me a simpleton. Of course, I'll be cautious."

"I don't think you're stupid, Jenny. I just think you're acting without thinking," Mason said.

His words stung Jenny. "In other words, you think I'm reckless."

"Yes. You're letting your feelings cloud your judgment."

She stepped up to him, her gaze locked on his. "You're wrong. But, while we're discussing feelings, I'm hurt that you think so little of me. You profess to love me, yet you don't think I'm being rational."

Mason took her by the upper arms. "Look, I know how smart you are, but..."

Jenny shook off his hands. "But nothing! You've made your feelings quite clear. I'm through with this discussion. I'm going to help Cecilia with dinner."

Frustration burned through Mason as Jenny exited the barn. He didn't want to argue with her, but he knew that

Andy wasn't to be trusted. He felt terrible about the Franklin kids, but he wasn't sure what could be done about it. As he groomed Jenny's horse, he prayed that Josh would be able to make headway with Andy.

Cecilia had just served dessert after a tense supper when someone knocked on the kitchen door.

Herb got up to answer it. "Well, Josh. Good to see you. Come on in."

Josh entered the kitchen, a tense expression on his face. "Evening, everyone." His dark eyes found Jenny. "Mrs. Crawford, uh, the young... I mean..."

Jenny smiled. "Just call me Jenny, Sheriff. That will avoid any confusion."

"All right. Thanks, Jenny," Josh said. "I paid the Franklins a visit, and I saw what you meant about the kids having bruises and all."

Jenny stood up. "Are you going to arrest Andy?"

Regret shone in Josh's eyes. "No, ma'am. Mrs. Franklin took Andy's side and swore that it was a misunderstanding. I can't press charges without a witness."

"I'm a witness!" Jenny insisted.

Mason rose to his feet. "Jenny, I'm sure Josh did all he could."

Josh shook his head. "Unless you saw Andy do it, you're

not a witness. I don't believe Mrs. Franklin, but my hands are tied. I gave Andy a stern warning, but unless she or the kids come forward, I'm pretty powerless. They weren't willing to go against him."

Tears welled in Jenny's eyes. "*Something* must be done."

Mason shared his wife's feelings, but he didn't see a solution. If Josh, a lawman, couldn't remedy the problem, then what could *he* do?

"I'll keep an eye on the situation," Josh said. "And if you see anything else or come up with any ideas, let me know. Sorry I didn't have better news."

Jenny swallowed her anger and sorrow. "I understand. Thank you, Sheriff."

Josh bid them farewell and they all returned to their seats. Jenny pushed her pie around on her plate but couldn't eat it. After a few moments, she said, "Excuse me," and left the table.

Cecilia turned to Mason. "Did you two have a disagreement?"

Mason scrubbed a hand over his face. "Yes. I'm going to go talk to her."

He followed Jenny to where she sat on the porch outside. She brushed away a tear as he came to stand next to her.

"Have you come to gloat?"

Her accusation stung. "Of course not. I was hoping Josh would be able to reach Andy. Those kids don't deserve what's happening to them."

Jenny glanced at him and the pain in her eyes tore at him. "No, they don't." She made an angry gesture. "He has his wife and children trapped. He's the one controlling their finances, so there's no way Mrs. Franklin can get away from him and have enough money to finish raising her children. Even if she did, she would be shunned for leaving him because society says that a man and woman must stay married no matter what."

Jenny tried to rein in her turbulent emotions, but she couldn't seem to shut her mouth. "No matter how much torture and pain a man metes out, his wife is powerless against him. She is forced to endure whatever treatment of her he sees fit."

Mason said, "Not all men are like that, Jenny. I'm not like that. Most men aren't."

Her smile as she faced him wasn't one of agreement. "Of course, you're not. You and Herb are good, decent men, but even men like you expect their wives to *obey* them. You're very unhappy with me over this because I just won't let the matter alone."

"Only because I…"

"Don't want me to be hurt. Yes, I know," Jenny interjected. "But I also think that it wouldn't do for the head of the town council's wife to be seen meddling in other people's affairs. Isn't that part of it? Or perhaps the main reason?"

Mason couldn't deny that it had crossed his mind. "It's

not the main reason, but I do have a responsibility to the community. And people won't listen to me if they don't approve of you."

"I think many people would approve of the school-teacher protecting children."

"That's not how everyone will see it, Jenny. How people raise kids is a personal thing, and they don't cotton to someone sticking their nose where it doesn't belong," Mason said.

Jenny recoiled at his statement. He'd unwittingly repeated what Andy had said to her in the mercantile. "So, you think I should just keep out of it?"

Her blue eyes blazed with anger and Mason regretted his words. "No. I think you should do what Josh said and let him handle it. He's the law here, not you."

"Mr. Franklin is lucky I'm not the law because I would've given him a taste of his own medicine. How I wish I did have brute strength on my side!" Jenny said. "However, that's not the case, so I'll just do whatever I can to help them. And don't worry. I won't embarrass you. I'm going to bed. Goodnight."

Jenny walked into the house before any more angry words could tumble out of her mouth.

THE SITUATION between Mason and Jenny caused a great

deal of tension between them. This wasn't helped when the Franklin children stopped attending school. Guilt tore at Jenny because she knew it was her fault. Perhaps if she'd restrained herself, she could've found another way to help Ethan and his siblings.

But the emotional side of her knew that she couldn't have resisted stepping in when she'd overheard Andy threatening Ethan. It just wasn't in her nature to stand by in the face of such cruelty. She longed to go to the Franklin ranch to see how the kids were faring, but she knew it would only make matters worse.

One night, a week after the Franklin children had last been in school, Jenny sat at her dressing table, brushing her hair. Mason stood at the washstand in their room, cleaning up after the long day. In her mirror, she followed the progress of the washcloth he used as it glided across his muscular chest.

Despite her displeasure with Mason, her hunger for him hadn't diminished. He turned and their eyes met in the mirror.

"Jenny, how long is this going to go on?" he asked.

Tears took her by surprise, clogging her throat. After a few moments, Jenny said, "You were right, Mason. I made things worse. The Franklin children still haven't returned to school."

Mason came and knelt by her side. "I don't want to be

right, Jenny. This has never been about that. I love you and it would kill me if you came to any harm."

His sincerity was reflected in his expression and Jenny felt her anger and resentment fade away. "I'm sorry that I didn't listen to you."

Mason tucked a stray lock of hair behind her ear. "I'm sorry that I didn't support you a little more about this. I never meant to hurt you."

"I believe you, Mason. I know what a good man you are. I *did* let my emotions get the best of me," Jenny said.

Mason smiled. "Don't be so hard on yourself. You caring so much is a good thing. And for the record, I don't think you're my property and I don't want you to obey me. We should work together to solve problems, not let them divide us."

"You're right," Jenny agreed. "We have to learn to listen to each other and not focus on who's wrong or right."

Mason pulled her close. "You know, I married a really smart woman."

Jenny smiled against his chest. "Yes, you did."

Mason's laugh rumbled under her ear, making her grin.

"And I married a very smart, not to mention, handsome man."

"I'm glad you think so." Mason kissed her forehead. "I love you, Jenny, and we're going to figure out how to help Andy's wife and kids. I don't know how yet, but we will."

Warmth flooded Jenny's heart, and she looked him in the

eyes. "Thank you so much, Mason. That means the world to me."

"I'll do anything for you, Jenny," Mason said.

Jenny sent him a coy smile. "There is something I'd like you to do for me."

"Which is?"

"Get up off your knee and then make love to me."

Her request sent desire coursing through Mason. He promptly rose and held out a hand to her. "Come to bed, honey."

Jenny complied, eager to be in his arms again. As he laid down with her, she pressed a kiss to his lips. "I love you so much, Mason. So much."

Mason didn't answer Jenny with words. Instead, as the moon outside rose higher, he showed her how much he cherished her. And later, when their passion was fully spent, Mason held her close as they caught their breath.

"Want to know what I love most about you?" he asked.

Jenny snuggled against his chest. "Yes. Tell me."

"Your big heart and fiery spirit," Mason said. "I never know what you're gonna do and you're never boring."

Jenny's shoulders shook with laughter. "I confess that I've always had a bit of a temper."

"Well, most people do, but what I meant was that you have so much life in you," Mason stated. "I love how much you care about people and that you stand up for them."

"Thank you." She lifted her head to meet his eyes. "I

don't want to fight like this again. Promise me that we'll talk about our problems right away and not let bad feelings fester."

Mason kissed the tip of her nose. "I promise. Now, get some rest."

Jenny cuddled against him with a smile at his seemingly bossy remark and drifted into slumber.

EPILOGUE

*A*few nights later, the Crawfords were playing cards when they heard a horse trot up to the house. Cecilia opened the door to find Josh Ryder on the porch.

"Come in, Sheriff. What can we do for you?" she asked.

Josh took off his hat as he stepped inside and greeted everyone. "I just wanted to tell you that I have Andy Franklin in custody." He looked at Jenny. "You were right. Andy was abusing Stella and the kids. She couldn't take it anymore and came to my office around noon to file charges. I deputized one of my friends and we brought Andy in. I've sent for the circuit judge to come to hear the case. Andy will stay locked up until then."

Blinking back tears, Jenny said, "I'm very sorry that I was correct in this circumstance but so happy that he can't hurt them any longer. I'll call on them tomorrow to see how I can help them. Thank you for letting us know, Josh."

He smiled. "You're welcome."

Mason and Jenny walked him out to his horse and saw him off. Jenny smiled when Mason slid his arms around her waist from behind and said, "I'm so glad that Stella turned him in."

"Me, too, but I do worry how they're going to get along without someone to work the farm for them," Jenny said. "I want to help them however I can."

He squeezed her a little. "You won't have to do it alone, honey." Turning in his arms, Jenny gave him a peck on the cheek. "What was that for, my fiery lady?"

"For being the most wonderful husband on Earth."

Mason laughed. "Well, I try." Suddenly sobering, he said, "I want to work together on solving problems, Jenny. Not just helping other people, but in our life together, too."

"I want the same thing," she said.

Mason smiled. "Good. Then that's how it's going to be. You and me, always working as a team."

"Always?" Jenny asked.

Mason gave a brief nod. "Always."

They shared a tender, leisurely kiss that sealed their vow, and they were secure in the knowledge that they could work through whatever difficulties life brought their way.

The End

CHARACTER LIST

- Mason Crawford, rancher
- Jenny Carson, schoolteacher
- Aunt Cecilia, Mason's aunt
- Uncle Herb, Mason's uncle
- Damon Frost, owner of the Station
- Maggie Frost, Damon's wife
- Elmarie Harmon, flower seller
- Mrs Timmons, visitor. Children: Gary
- Ted Drayton, stagecoach driver
- Nell Danvers, waitress
- Liddy Bentley, cheesemaker
- Eli Carson, Jenny's brother
- Paul Gibbons, pastor
- Andy and Stella Franklin, ranchers. Children: Ethan, Lenny, Betty

- Josh Ryder, sheriff

AMELIA'S OTHER BOOKS

Montana Westward Brides

#0 The Rancher's Fiery Bride

#1 The Reckless Doctor's Bride

#2 The Rancher's Unexpected Pregnant Bride

#3 The Lonesome Cowboy's Abducted Bride

#4 The Sheriff's Stubborn Secretive Bride

Bear Creek Brides

#1 The Rescued Bride's Savior

#2 A Faithful Bride For The Wounded Sheriff

#3 The Untangling of Two Hearts

#4 Indian Bride for the Trusty Miner

#5 Quick-Witted Bride for the Troubled Doctor

#6 A Loving Heart for the Loyal Deputy

#7 The Pastor's Doubtful Bride

#8 Warming a Cold Heart

#9 A Division of the Heart

#10 The Rancher's Abducted Bride

#11 Healing a Self-Conscious Woman's Heart

#12 Winning Her Guarded Heart

Daisy Creek Brides

#1 Scarred Mail Order Bride and the Widower

CONNECT WITH AMELIA

Visit my website at **www.ameliarose.info** to view my other books and to sign up to my mailing list so that you are notified about my new releases and special offers.

ABOUT AMELIA ROSE

Amelia is a shameless romance addict with no intentions of ever kicking the habit. Growing up she dreamed of entertaining people and taking them on fantastical journeys with her acting abilities, until she came to the realization as a college sophomore that she had none to speak of. Another ten years would pass before she discovered a different means to accomplishing the same dream: writing stories of love and passion for addicts just like herself. Amelia has always loved romance stories and she tries to tie all the elements she likes about them into her writing.

COPYRIGHT

Made in the USA
Middletown, DE
25 March 2021